THE MOSQUITO-BITE AUTHOR

EMERGING VOICES FROM THE MIDDLE EAST

Series Editor
Dena Afrasiabi

Other titles in this series include:
Wûf
Dying in a Mother Tongue
Using Life
Limbo Beirut

THE MOSQUITO-BITE AUTHOR

by **BARIŞ BIÇAKÇI**
Translated by **MATTHEW CHOVANEC**

CENTER FOR MIDDLE EASTERN STUDIES
The University of Texas at Austin

Cover Design by Sam Strohmeyer
Book Design by Allen Griffith of Eye 4 Design

Library of Congress Control Number: 2020942214
ISBN: 978-1477321096

THE MOSQUITO-BITE AUTHOR

Most of the time you can see things coming. Miracle, the old house cat, is going to die today or tomorrow. He's been sleeping in the corner all day long without moving. We want him to wake up, but just look at the poor thing, he should keep sleeping.

Relationships between humans and cats are complicated, Cemil thinks to himself.

"The doctors here are terrible!" his dad says, "let's go to another hospital."

Twenty years ago, when Cemil had gone into his father's room at the hospital, he had found him dressed in bright blue pajamas, sitting on the bed and checking his pulse. He had a worried look on his face. His thumb was pressed against his wrist, his head turned slightly to the side, looking at his wristwatch. His face was shiny with sweat, as if he were fighting against something more powerful than himself. The numbers were moving on his lips.

"What's going on, Dad, what are you doing?" Cemil asked, but it was a pointless question; he knew right away what was going on: his dad wanted to live.

"Why are you taking your pulse?"

"I don't trust the doctors or the nurses around here! They said they've gotten my blood pressure down but it hasn't dropped. Don't they think I know myself?" He put the palm of his hand on top of his head. "I have a burning sensation here, like it's burning inside. Let's go to another hospital."

"Don't be silly, Dad! They've done so many tests, they looked at everything...They did all the prep work . . . and you'll have an operation in a day or two . . . where are you getting this idea of going to another hospital from!" Regardless of what was going to happen, Cemil just wished he could turn back time to a moment earlier; to that moment there waiting with his father, to his pain, his life, he wanted to draw it all out. "What does your blood pressure or pulse have to do with anything, Dad?" But they do have something to do with it! The thought of death makes everything seem connected to everything else, setting up the circuitry and lighting up the dusty lightbulbs of fear.

Cemil picked up the pink folder from the top of the radiator and gave it a look. The pink color felt out of place, but all the colors in the room felt out of place, like laughter at the inopportune moment.

"They just took your blood pressure half an hour ago. One 'o five over sixty-seven." The number was good. Cemil didn't think the number was cause for concern, it was a relief even. He began speaking with a soft, calming voice. He even made a joke: "you have the blood pressure of a young girl, Dad!"

His father gave a forced smile. His arms were down at his side, his head tilted forward. Cemil was only accustomed to his father's immense strength, a strength he once felt in the tightly shut faucet handles at home, but now he didn't have the strength to do anything anymore.

He took a napkin out of the packet on top of the nightstand and wiped his father's forehead. He stroked his head. He blew lightly on a thin gray hair. He grasped his ears, which seemed like they had grown a little bit; larger and sagging. A retired history teacher's large, sagging ears. There were definitely more spots on his forehead than there used to be. Behind his glasses his eyelids were red and puffy, he looked unhealthy, and his thinning eyelashes suddenly made Cemil feel strangely sad. Sadness is always there hiding in the most unexpected places.

Cemil was about to cry; he turned and looked out the window. But he didn't see anything but the low hanging clouds arranged in a line by the March wind and the large wide row of uniform hospital buildings.

Ground, sky, hospital. The windows were multiplying, making copies of themselves, spreading out in every direction. Cemil rubbed his eyes. The windows were all still there. There were plastic bags full of food hanging out of most of them. There were milk bottles and yoghurt containers perched on the ledges.

"Aren't you ashamed?" his father asked.

Cemil stuttered "wh-what for?"

His father didn't answer; Cemil didn't press him on it. Father and son with their heads both looking ahead. A touching portrait of genetics. It was getting dark outside, it was getting even harder to make out the thing that was keeping them there. In the silence and stillness Cemil thought that he was as close to death as his father was. They were both going to die. Yes. Two men at the end of the road, for whom not even poetry was of any use. Poetry acts as a kind of remedy for death, especially that final verse and the rhyme that digs in with its claws.

"Now, when that door opens, if it's a pretty woman who walks in . . ." his father said.

Cemil looked confused as the door slowly opened, held open wide enough for a stretcher to fit through.

"A beautiful woman with a bubbly personality."

He wasn't holding out for the best doctor in the world to walk in, equipped with the newest developments in medicine, but instead for a beautiful woman. And he was saying it in such a calm way that Cemil knew what he meant: a woman bringing the declaration that would clear him of any wrongdoing, the stay of his execution right before it was to be carried out. She would come in through that door, approaching with small steps, and when she leaned over to hand him the document she would show off her breasts (check your pulse now, Dad!) and everything would be different. That's what his father wanted.

We want so many things from women, Cemil thought to himself. To forgive us, to show us their breasts, to make us immortal.

His father wasn't saying anything. He had died twenty-two years ago, long since unable to muster that rational approach to things that only the living possess. Now he would butt in whenever he felt like it, showing up at random. Another trait often found in the dead.

Miracle, Cemil says to himself, our old cat, if only the hospital room door would open and a beautiful woman would walk in!

2

The publishing house manager asked Cemil when he had gotten to Istanbul. He was smiling. Cemil pointed to his backpack and said "this morning." Then he scratched his cheek with the tip of his index finger.

When someone from Istanbul talks to someone from Ankara, they're always smiling. Like you've just said something stupid or childish, or like they're put off by how you're acting, scratching your cheek even though it doesn't itch.

"Let me explain how things work here," the manager said, "you'll want to know the process."

He started to explain. While the manager spoke, Cemil felt like some inexperienced idiot looking for a job, remembering the nerve-wracking interviews he had gone on years ago. He was overcome with a feeling of defeat. This is so stupid! He thought about crossing his legs, or putting his arm on the back of the chair in order to feel more comfortable, but those awkward memories were still just an arm's length away. Sitting right there.

The manager said that dozens of manuscripts came to the publishing house every month, and that most of them were rejected by the editor after the first few pages. "Writers who've never typed on a computer before. They can't even come up with one decent sentence!" he said. "You can imagine what kinds of ridiculous things we get." He laughed. Cemil laughed too.

The room's two walls were packed floor to ceiling with bookshelves. There were more than one thousand books that the publishing house had printed, neatly organized on the shelves and lit up by the March sun. While looking at this happy family portrait, Cemil thought to himself how those books, along with other nice things, made him feel like a loser. Those books were signs of accomplishment, of things that had been finished. Life, on the other hand, was full of things that were left unaccomplished and unfinished. You're out there drowning in the surf, while literatis sun themselves on the seashore, sipping at their *mates*. It would be *mate* of course: that literary flourish invented by the Latin Americans.

The manager watched silently for a while as Cemil stared at the books, and then asked him how old he was. He was surprised to learn that Cemil was forty-five, saying he looked much younger. He asked him what the secret to staying young was. Cemil explained how he had quit after working for twelve years in construction, and had been living at home for nine years, living a slow, peaceful life. "To tell the truth, my wife is taking care of me now," he said, "and she's a doctor so she's pretty good at it too." The manager laughed. "And once a week I go play indoor soccer. Tuesdays . . ." Cemil added. The manager asked which position he played. It was normal protocol for a sophisticated urban male to be seen taking indoor soccer matches seriously. But he wasn't very interested in Cemil's answer, "kids?" he then asked, "you don't have any kids?"

Cemil said he didn't want any kids, "of course it's hard for women to make that decision," he said, looking off in the distance with an expression of seriousness. The manager nodded, smiling, and with a gesture of his hand made it clear he wanted to change the subject, "I'm guessing this is the first thing you've written, your first novel," he said. Cemil explained that he had struggled to write poetry when he was twenty but had never gotten the hang of it and had dropped it. "Poetry's hard...Poetry's hard!" The manager said, "Plus no one reads it anymore. Come, I'll introduce you to our editor who'll be looking at your manuscript."

Cemil followed after the manager, wearing his backpack and holding the manuscript in his hand. They went up to another floor. As the manager opened a door painted navy blue, he laughed, saying "here's our workshop!" Cemil promised himself that he wouldn't laugh at any more of the manager's cheap jokes. "You're not a dandelion seed, you're a forty-five-year-old man."

They entered a room full of people, desks, chairs, computers, printers, and cables. Two men sat talking in front of a big computer screen; one of them turned and smiled at Cemil. They passed by a woman putting her glasses down on her desk, trying to tell whether or not its temples were crooked. A piece of biscuit that a middle-aged man had dipped into his cup of tea softened and fell off into his lap before he could get it to his mouth; a mid-life crisis. A young man spun his pen up into the air and caught it. A young redhead started cutting, with scissors, a big manila envelope with an address written on it.

The manager, introducing Cemil to the editor, said "I explained the process to Mr. Cemil, now you can speak to one another in your own lingo." Pleased with himself, he pointed at the manuscript Cemil was holding in his hand. Cemil put the folder down on the editor's desk. As the manager went to leave he stretched out his hand to Cemil and said "right, I hope we'll see each other again."

The editor reached for the phone. "you want some tea?"

"I had some with Mr. Selim, thanks. My stomach doesn't really like when I drink tea back to back." He hadn't eaten breakfast. Because of that, and because of the excitement, he had stomach cramps.

"You can't make literature if you're feeling raw!" the editor said.

Cemil rubbed against the chair he was sitting in like his back was itching, moved his shoulders, and said "for sure . . .", caught unprepared. He had just been looking off at the redhead girl he had passed. The girl was collecting up the little sticky note sized pieces of the envelope she had cut up and was putting them into a small cardboard box.

"Without some feeling being balanced by another violent, intense feeling . . ." the editor paused for a moment, looking for just the right expression, rubbing her thumb and forefinger together quickly a few times. "without feelings mixing with others in the right mix you can't make literature!" she said. Cemil realized that the editor often resorted to this "I'm looking for just the right expression" theatricality. Just like the manager had predicted, they were understanding each other in their own special lingo. The editor rubbed her fingers together and pursed her lips. When you think about it, without the right expression, you'll be off on the wrong foot, left worrying about falling off a cliff.

The editor gave an example from her own life: "It's like curing an olive in salt. The salt takes the bitterness away."

Cemil interjected "Gemlik olives! That's what I call that kind of olives."

"There's also a danger with aphorism!" The editor said.

Aphorism . . . that thick white substance we spread over our bread at breakfast. It's not nutritious, but it is filling. "Right!" said Cemil.

"In this day and age, too many writers' books are nothing more than a collection of aphorisms. We no longer find a unique world inside books and stories." She rubbed her fingers together. "Sentences which can easily be shared . . . It's too bad that literature is turning into easily circulating sentences. People are in pursuit of expressions they can write and say to one another. It's wearing out even the most sophisticated readers."

The editor wasn't saying this spitefully; to the contrary she sounded kind of indifferent. She was doing her job. She picked up Cemil's manuscript from the desk and read the name of the novel. She smiled and said "you've picked an interesting title." She turned to his left, "but as you can see, there's a lot of manuscripts that have to get read, it will take some time to give you the good or bad news."

Cemil had to stretch his head back around to look at the place the editor was showing him. On top of an end table he saw dozens of multi-colored, various-sized files stacked on top of each other in a pile. "Yes, Mr. Selim mentioned that," he said. He didn't want to pass up the opportunity to show off just how much patience, that most writerly of virtues, he in fact possessed. "I waited years to write, I can wait for it to get published too."

But the sight of all of those manuscripts was really terrible, they looked like they'd never made a single movement or sound. They weren't covered in dust, but they still made you want to blow on them, shake them, smack them. Smack them with the palm of your hand. Let all those words settle to the ground; make the manuscripts' owners come to their senses, stop them from getting carried away with their silly fantasies.

3

After giving his novel manuscript to the publisher, Cemil walked through the crowd on Istiklal Caddesi. In one of the shops on the street he ate something between breakfast and lunch. After going as far as Taksim he turned back around towards Tünel. He made his way down to Karaköy via backstreets. He crossed over to Kadıköy on the ferry. He tried calling his friends in Istanbul, then gave up. He walked around the streets of Moda. He sat in a tea garden. The tea was really good, the sea looked really beautiful. He wanted to head right back home, to Nazlı. He bought a ticket for the first bus to Ankara. In the middle of the night he arrived at his apartment complex, built thirty kilometers outside of the city. He pushed aside the shopping cart left at the bottom of the entrance stairs in front of the apartment building. He climbed silently up to the fourth floor. Inside the dark apartment, he listened to Nazlı's breathing. He took a shower. He got into bed.

When I leave my own world I become the subject of simple sentences, he thought to himself, and then embraced Nazlı and started to go over the vague edges of a picture; when he came to the end he realized it wasn't a picture but rather a beautiful, complex sentence. A beautiful, complex sentence.

The sound of two hundred and fifty grams of hazelnuts being poured
into a glass jar . . . At first the sound of a baby's laugh, then it turned
into a beautiful sentence; Cemil wrote that down in his journal.
The journal was full of beautiful sentences.

Cemil had wanted other sentences that would rotate around these
beautiful sentences without really knowing what those other sentences would do, and that's what he got. The mechanics of heavenly
bodies. Everything revolves ceaselessly around something else, an
intoxication from which mankind takes its fair share.

Cemil had gotten drunk. He told Nazlı that he wanted to write a
novel about the songs they had listened to when they were young,
the time that had passed, and life itself, which had gone on despite
everything. Nazlı got excited. He looked like he was going to say
something but instead just took a couple of sips one right after
another. He closed his eyes. When he opened them again, Cemil had
an expression on his face like that of a person who picks up a pen
with the need to record not only what had happened to them, but
the great rush of all things. But he couldn't make it down past the
top of his notebook. He confused day and nighttime, two nights on
one side of the scale and one day on the other. Sleeplessness made
him edgy, the thin leaf of sleep inside his rib cage. Sentences that
in other times would have never come to him, coming out in a
turmoil as they smashed against the shoreline. All of Cemil's habits
changed. He didn't have breakfast consistently, ate lunch on his feet,
spooning out Nazlı's food from the pot or eating canned tuna with a
spoon. Except for the weekly indoor soccer games, he didn't leave
the apartment complex. During games he ran eagerly after the ball

and it was as if it was the first time since puberty that he had so eagerly pursued something real.

He kept writing without fully realizing that it was what he had dreamt about doing for years, the thing he imagined would turn him into another person, someone more in command of their own life. He was quickly making progress. He was like a lonely old woman who puts her knitting materials into a plastic bag and heads outside when the sun comes out: he wanted to tell the story of everything he had lived.

He believed that he would explain the world with a special, mathematical elegance and precision.

Then, all of a sudden, the elegance and precision were lost. Cemil thought the things he had written were cheap and fake. "I'm being an idiot!" he said to himself. He grew sullen. He looked at the spider patiently waiting for its prey in its web, strung up between the washing machine and the shower tray. He stopped writing. He felt like he had committed a crime; not for having stopped writing, but for having tried to write in the first place. He started reading *Ada or Ardor*. After a little bit, the brilliant book made him forget his feelings of defeat. Literature . . . it was the end of June. One morning when he went out to get the paper, Cemil saw some tough looking guys walking around, smelling the branches of the silverberry tree they had torn off. Cemil was chased by two noisy magpies trying to protect their nest, and when he got home he picked up writing where he had left off. As he wrote, he understood that emotional tides were an inevitable part of life. A sentence he wrote on one day he would hate the next. On one day he would have total faith, the next day he would think about all that was going on in the country, and feel that it was truly unethical to write a character without much of a connection to the world. Then he thought that because the world was already the way it was, writing was the one ethical option left: a person with a pen can only do harm to themselves. Sometimes he read what he had written, and when he wasn't satisfied with some things he would change the parts in the first person to the third person, making the male characters female, the female characters male, then put everything back the way that it was: a kind of primordial soup. The source of all biological and literary existence.

Nazlı would make lemonade by stirring together lemon peels and sugar, bringing it along with some crackers, singing folk songs in her beautiful voice, and then suddenly get annoyed and angry at Cemil for spending all of his time and attention on writing a book. Dealing with Nazlı and dealing with literature increasingly resembled one another.

Cemil finished *Ada or Ardor* at the beginning of September. The thing that happened whenever he finished books happened again: it was like someone changed the water in his aquarium. It took time to get used to the new water. During this time, the connection to reality was interrupted. It felt like Nazlı was the only thing in the world, but he even slightly doubted she was real. In order to remove his doubt when he was at the desk at home during the day he would suddenly say Nazlı's name out loud. At night he would press his crotch up against Nazlı's life giving hips.

When December came around, he finished his novel. He began transferring what he had written to his computer. He changed around many more things at this point as well. He felt like the novel was going to run a little long. He distracted himself with other things. During the week of New Years, they went to the city where Nazlı's parents lived. They watched a lot of television. When they got home, Cemil had suddenly become addicted to several shows. He'd even eagerly watch the preview for the next episode once the show was over. He saw a lot of his friends Metin and İlhan. He did a few small repair jobs around the apartment. Some days he'd go to the hospital and eat lunch with Nazlı.

In March he went back to his desk and, in a habit left over from when he wrote poetry, he read the novel out loud from start to finish. He changed the parts that sounded awkward. Then it sounded like music. A few notes . . . a few drops . . .

"Alright!" he said, emphasizing the last syllable. He wanted Nazlı to read what he had written. He circled around her during the evenings while she was reading it. He looked into her eyes. It got on his nerves a few times when he felt like she was reading too quickly. He asked her if she understood. Whenever Nazlı laughed or cried while she was reading, Cemil would laugh or cry too. When Nazlı finished the novel, she said "while I was reading, it was like I was close to the ground but also like I was flying . . . yes, that's what it was like!" She inflated her chest, took a deep breath. She stood up in an extremely emotional and serious way and kissed Cemil's hands. Someone looking in on them from outside would think they were both psychopaths. The vanity of a childless couple, hugging each other, showing a gratuitous amount of enthusiasm . . .

Cemil called the publisher in Istanbul in the middle of March to arrange a meeting to hand over the manuscript. That night, the sound of shouting came from outside. It woke Cemil and Nazlı up. They tried to figure out what it was. It sounded like women screaming, and like they were running, like they were trying to tell someone something. But they couldn't make out what was being said. Then the voices grew distant. But what Nazlı and Cemil had understood was enough to keep both of them awake until morning.

Two days later, as the bus to Istanbul drove on the access road right next to the apartment complex on its way to the highway, Cemil immediately recognized the heating station illuminated by bright lights on the hill out in the darkness, and looked excitedly at the first-stage apartment blocks surrounding it, lit up by their own remote lights.

Like watching the earth from space.

5

Towards the end of the nineteen eighties, construction began on an apartment complex located between the highway to Ayaş and the highway to Istanbul. The workers who had come to set up worksite tents looked on in admiration at the wide landscape of low-lying, rolling hills and fields sown with grain. One of them, looking at the chaff of the grain, said that it would be a good harvest. Another one of them agreed. The land was fertile, the grain was tall. As they went over towards a reed bed on the side of the Istanbul Highway, they saw a small lake fed by rainwater. One of them said that the water was a blessing, the others agreed. They were in the middle of the steppe, and other than the Ankara stream, poisoned and flowing to its slow death out towards the West a few kilometers to the south of them, there was nothing else resembling water. The workers took their supplies off the truck and set up their worksite camps and prefab structures. They told each other about their childhoods in the village, their youth. In the threshing area, sitting cross-legged around the ox-pulled thrasher, they spoke about their dreams. Their eyes were also fixed on the ox's tail. Was the animal raising its tail like it was about to go to the bathroom? They would rush to pick up two handfuls of hay from the ground and hold it up to the ox's bottom so that the animals would go the other way and not crap on the wheat kernels. The workers' conversations couldn't be heard over the noise of the trucks carrying building materials, the mechanical diggers excavating the foundation, and the cement mixers. They set up a large crane tower. They poured cement into the tunnel formwork. Floors went up over the plinth wall. Scaffolding and a pulley system were installed. The workers made tea in the corners of the doorless, windowless buildings. The tea cups were held up towards the sun as they looked at the steeped tea. They told each other stories about men

BARIŞ BIÇAKÇI

they knew who were experts at brewing tea. They made roads around and between the buildings, dug ditches to run the electric cables, water, natural gas and pipes for central heating systems. Cabinetmakers and glass cutters went into the five or ten story buildings. They hung up doors in the apartments. Fitters ran cables and pipes inside of the buildings. They installed bathtubs and toilets, squat toilet slabs, sinks, shower trays, wash basins. They spread bitumen over the PVC pipe. The tile workers laid tile, did joint work. During the holidays, those who could would travel back home. Those who couldn't would shave and then head down to Ulus and Kızılay. When they got back, they installed kitchen cabinets and countertops. To hide the pipes going towards the bathtubs and toilets they hung up dropped ceilings from wide aluminum strips. They mounted electric plug sockets and switches. Some of the workers bought cologne and went to visit their friends who had been injured in work accidents in the hospital. Without telling one another that their friends wouldn't be able to work anymore, that it would be impossible to find another job, the carpet makers would come and start installing cheap wall to wall carpet. The apartment doors, numbers, and name signs were hung up. Transformer buildings, work centers, schools, post offices, police stations, and lunch counters were built. Market stalls, parks, playgrounds were set up. The workers would call home from the telephone booths located in front of the post office. After asking how all of their relatives were doing, they would tell them that the Prime Minister was going to officiate the opening of the first phase of the building, and then say that they were guaranteed work for at least two or three more years.

He boiled water. Was it the water that Cemil had been waiting for? In truth, it was news from the publisher that he was waiting for since the day, the hour he had dropped off his manuscript. He covered the bottom part of the kettle and steeped the tea. Then he lit the small stove, using his hand to lightly jiggle the connection to the oven to get the flames to come out of all of its holes. Once the little blue flames formed a complete circle, he placed the kettle on top of them. The water began to boil and then there across from him was Oktay Rifat: *The boiling teapot is a scented tree planted in the kitchen.* Poets love to appear subtly and humbly in this way.

While Cemil waited for the tea to boil, but really for news from the publisher, he looked out the window. There were pigeons strutting about on the rooftops and balconies, jerkily turning their heads. The black bands on their wings, the light gray colors waving on their necks . . . one of the temporary forms that existence takes in this universe. Matter coming together in the form of a bird. One could say the same about us, ask about the human soul, but what could anyone say! Humans couldn't tolerate being nothing more than a body, that was clear, Cemil thought. So much so that we had to invent something called a soul because we were unable to cope with just having bodies. A pretty brilliant idea to be honest!

As Cemil poured the tea, he noticed that the white porcelain teapot lid and corners had darkened over the years. These kinds of things catch the eye and then life feels soiled, stained so to speak. But big things can come about from these simple observations. That's how we got bleach. Nazlı sometimes soaked the teapot in bleach.

After breakfast he vacuumed. Seeing the dusty floor made spotless after the vacuum cleaner was run over it, hearing the rattling noise of debris being sucked into the tube into the vacuum's dirt chamber, it all made Cemil happy. It was also great when he pressed the button on the vacuum and the cord wound back up automatically.

Around noon, he sat in his chair and read a few pages of *The Heart is a Lonely Hunter*, which he had started before going to the interview with the publisher in Istanbul. The book was really good, but at that precise moment he couldn't get into it. Even though it had only been two days, he kept wondering if the publisher would call or not, and if they did call, when it would be.

He stared at the telephone.

He called the apartment complex manager. Old Mrs. Fatma picked up. She complained about having back pain. The apartment on the top floor had been vacated; they said they were getting too much sunlight. She asked about Nazlı. "Thank you, young man, for calling me like this. You and Nazlı should come over for dinner one night," she said.

The number for management was close to the one for old Mrs. Fatma. Cemil called management. He listened patiently to the voice recording saying that the call might be monitored for security purposes. After that, the woman on duty picked up, saying "Management!"

"I wanted to ask about what I can do with my piles of old magazines," Cemil said. There was a pause. "There used to be an environmental group that came and took them, but they don't do that anymore." There was another pause. "There are a bunch of magazines sitting in the storehouse. Maybe management could help out, offer a suggestion? I mean, if you were the ones who used to pick them up is what I'm saying." The woman answered in a way that made it clear she didn't care very much about the problem: "garbage collection is up to you now, that's the way it is! Ask the security guard, maybe they can help." They told each other to have a nice day then hung up.

The phone rang in the afternoon.

Metin said, "I heard from Nazlı that you're back." He asked how the interview at the publisher went. He was curious why Cemil had come back so quickly: "Weren't you going to stay for a little bit?" Cemil described the conversation with the editor. "We didn't really speak a lot about literature. Well I didn't speak much to be honest . . . wasn't really a need to . . ." He said that he had decided not to stay in Istanbul, that when he was away from home he felt like he had been pushed out of his own life. He made a comparison between Istanbul and Ankara. Everyone who goes to Istanbul brings back a comparison with them, just like they would Turkish delight, or floss halva, saray helva, Bolçi chocolates. "In Istanbul it seems like everyone's sole aim is to savour Istanbul. They look like a predator who has its eyes set on its prey. You couldn't see your prey in Ankara even if you wanted to, there are too many pedestrian crossings in the way." He laughed together with Metin at this joke. When they hung up, Cemil said "When I was walking around in Istanbul I felt sad for the state of the world. People in Ankara only get sad about the state of Ankara."

After talking to Metin, Cemil called İlhan. İlhan said he wasn't surprised that Cemil had come back early. "It's to be expected from you! You spend one day away, and the house loses your scent. You're rubbing yourself all over everything like a cat trying to get it back."

After speaking to İlhan he went to the store. He was too lazy to wash spinach, so he bought chard. Around evening, while he was making a big helping of rice with chard he got the creeps looking at the chard's wide, dark green leaves and veins. Biology can give you the creeps sometimes.

In the evening before Nazlı got home, he picked his book back up and sat in his chair. He got into it for a while, then sighed and looked over at the bookcase covering the opposite wall. The neck of the table lamp looked shadowy and enchanted in the contorted light. He gulped as he looked on. He got up and went over to the bookcase. As a flatter Cemil, squished in a literary sort of way, he would have fit in between *Bestiario* and *We Love Glenda So Much and Other Tales*. Then he became a piece of bric-a-brac. A sad clown in front of *Lolita*.

7

Nazlı knew that there was a sad clown waiting for her at home. She knew when she returned to the apartment and went up the stairs Cemil would have his ear pressed to the door and that as soon as she inserted the key he would open the door, smile and, with his pointer finger wagging, say "I got you!"

Sometimes Nazlı found him making dinner in the kitchen; mixing the tarhana soup with a wooden spoon, pulling the peeled eggplants out of the salt water bath, leaned over in front of the stove, turning the heat way down under the saucepan.

Nazlı also knew that Cemil had spent the entire day in the house struggling with his own mental unravelling. The house was full of the threads, filling up with the scraps, the loose ends of memories and ragged ideas unable to be joined together. Living in this small apartment had its flaws; there were lots of things that Cemil couldn't work on or complete in fifty-four square meters. There was silence. Silence arising from the thing he felt at that precise moment which he couldn't tell anyone. Silences, sips and dust he hid away in the corner.

When they sat down for dinner, Cemil first asked Nazlı what she had eaten for lunch, and then listened with interest as she explained stories about her patients and the hospital. Sometimes he listened like it was the real world, sometimes like it was imaginary. Their home was the place where Cemil could let his guard down when it came to reality and his imagination.

Cemil also explained how his day had gone: a day he had spent entirely within the confines of the apartment complex. A day that had proceeded smoothly without any obstacles. Morning, afternoon, and evening.

"The bathtub in the upstairs apartment is leaking again, if it's still happening tomorrow I'm going to go let them know. I finished reading *Who's Looking Inside*. You should read it too, really strange, really beautiful. I took a walk in the afternoon. I got the things I needed from the store, but I couldn't find thyme water. Still no word from the publisher. How many weeks have gone by, I'm turning into a dead butterfly from waiting, stirring slightly in the wind like I'm still alive. In the afternoon, they fixed the speakers at the school. Testing, one two, testing. A kid came by selling toothpaste, pretended at first to be doing a survey on oral health. It was clear he didn't even convince himself. A university student. What are we going to do, Nazlı, how are we supposed to help people? Help all of them?

Nazlı knew quite well that Cemil was unenthusiastic about getting another job ever since he had resigned from his last one and started staying at home. She had even been supportive of his decision to quit. But she had initially hidden the fact from her family and work friends because they would have expected an explanation. Nazlı didn't want to give an explanation. Everything outside of the usual in this world requires an explanation and this requirement isn't at all innocent. You give an explanation, you explain the reasons why, you present reasonable justifications, then you realize that you're using the language of those expecting an explanation rather than your own. If you owe someone an explanation, you always pay the price by losing your own language.

Since childhood, Nazlı had been forced to explain all sorts of things to others. She was ashamed of the things she couldn't explain, and told lies. Even now, she was being made to explain why she was still living in a little box of an apartment despite making good money, why she didn't have a car, or didn't want to have kids, why she was married to a man who had suddenly quit his job at a large construction company where he was expected to rise his way up and who had begun staying at home. She only kept quiet. What a charming paradox: to preserve your own world and your own words by keeping quiet!

On the other hand, Nazlı felt angry at the medical profession, at the environment of the hospital, for making her remain quiet and bear Cemil's responsibilities, thinking that this sad clown had ruined his life. It distanced her from him. She was also annoyed that he had more ownership over the house than she did. But then a smile, a scent, the sight of Cemil's butt poking out from his briefs as he got up out of bed . . . no matter how much she didn't want to, she would feel close to him again. "My far away friend!" she would call out to Cemil, meaning the precise opposite. Because while love tries to be the primary emotion, it often gets mixed up with other things, peace of mind for example, or stability or balance. You make promises to yourself. In vain.

Nazlı also knew it was worthless to try to distance herself from Cemil. When she saw him sitting silently in his chair, looking at the bookcase, she wanted to insert herself and help this child who was afraid of books. She wanted to heal this sick child whose parents were on the edge of death; she felt responsible for protecting him from all death, and from every type of bad thing. When she put on a nice song, and Cemil got up out of his chair and started dancing like a vagabond, like he would stumble at any moment, whenever he started dancing like a streetlight, Nazlı would come out from the darkness and into the light of this streetlamp, and use it to search for the things she had lost.

From that height the only way down was to fall. Jazz artists have sad stories. With their fingers and their breath, they rise to the greatest heights possible: there's a change in temperature and pressure, the laws of common-sense shift, and the only way to get down from that height is by falling.

The trumpet player was a young guy in the middle of the stage, shot by a single bullet in the chest by a jealous lover. Writhing on the floor from side to side in the agony of death, he looked like a rattlesnake: that was the image they named the album after. Before dying, the last thing the trumpet player saw was the excessively swollen feet of the saxophonist. The saxophonist was a jokester, always saying "I want to get the sound of a dry martini to come out of my saxophone! That's all I'm going for." He was hitting middle-age, and had terribly swollen feet. His friends were advising him to go see a doctor. "Kidney cancer," the doctor said without hesitation, "quite an advanced stage." There was no use in the saxophone player making an effort anymore, death for him was already something cut and dry. The pianist looked at him and said "I can hear what you're playing but my ears don't believe it!" This was a compliment. Good, but a little late isn't it? "No, it's not too late," the pianist said, "especially since I'm already dead!" Good. When the doctor wrote the pianist's death certificate he couldn't believe his eyes: he was only thirty-five but looked sixty at least. The bassist was upset, leaving the doctor at home. On the way home the bassist's dog stuck its head out the window, smelling the air; the dog's ears flying in the wind. Then a loud noise, the dog had disappeared, the bassist had fallen and was lying bloody in a hedge at the side of a wide road. Somehow he was succeeding in making himself look bucktoothed, asking those who'd seen the accident and had come to help: "If I was

BARIŞ BIÇAKÇI

ugly like this would you still love me?" and before hearing the answer to his question he took his last breath. There isn't a sincere answer to that question anyways. The only one left was the drummer. His bones hurt like somebody had put a curse on him; he felt an unbearable pain in his joints. The drummer couldn't play. He left the drumsticks and tried to stand with great difficulty. Making his way toward the audience, he pulled out a handful of money from his pocket. "I don't deserve this!" he screamed. He threw the money in the air. There's a knock at the door . . . What? There's a knock at the door.

Cemil cuts off the sound of the music.

"Of course you can't hear the doorbell if you're listening to the music this loud!" says the woman at the door. Half of this takes place before Cemil opens the door, and half after opening it. Cemil immediately realizes that the woman hadn't said this to herself, but that she had said it to a man who was out of sight. That's the way it is in our country: when a man and a woman come face to face, there will always be a second man there as well, even if you can't see him.

"Your tub is leaking!" the woman says; pleased by the light nod of his head that Cemil had given to the man who was not there.

"Is it from the pipes, or maybe it's coming from the ground?"

"How would I know!" the woman says.

"In general it leaks from the floor but I didn't let any water leak on the floor . . . good Lord!"

"I swear it's leaking. My mother-in-law's house . . . come and see if you want."

Cemil took the two flashlights hanging from the side of the coat closet, took his slippers off and put on his shoes. He followed behind the woman and the out-of-sight man down the stairs.

Cemil had stepped up onto a stool in the middle of the bathroom,
ducking his head down so it wouldn't touch the drop ceiling. With a
flashlight in his hand . . . he looked ridiculous. He took a few of the
ceiling tiles out from their aluminum strips and placed them in the
shower tray; he poked his flashlight up into the space it created and
began inspecting the ceiling and pipes. The ceiling was covered with
asphalt. After the pipes came out from the ceiling they ran together
before connecting to the main pipe going down at a light slope next to
the door. Cemil inspected the pipes running to the sink in the kitchen,
the shower tray, the one connected to the hole on the floor of the
bathroom and the one coming from the toilet. As the flashlight lit up
this confusing black world, Cemil felt a strange delight. Then, on the
side of the hole on the bathroom floor, in a space full of rubble made
of a concrete and styrofoam mixture, he saw the water leaking. The
leaking water shined in the beam of the flashlight.

"It's coming from within the floor!" He said, bewildered, "I told you I
wasn't letting water leak onto the floor!" He pulled his head out from
the hole in the ceiling and looked towards the door from the stool.

Three women had poked their heads in and were looking at him
from the bathroom door. He noticed the old woman right away. She
was completely white, both her hair and her nightgown. She was
shaking her head. Mrs. Nermin from apartment five had also come in.
Most likely it had been the woman speaking to the out-of-sight man
who had called her.

"Hope it's going well Mr. Cemil!" Mrs. Nermin said.

A man on a stool and three women watching him. One of those
delightful moments in which life resembled a circus. Take a flying leap
Cemil!

BARIŞ BIÇAKÇI

"It's leaking from inside the floor," Cemil said.

"All the apartments are like this." Mrs. Nermin quickly began to explain:

"It's getting hard to get my mother into the tub to wash her. Sometimes I sit on the toilet and wash her like that. Of course, whenever I do, water gets on the floor and drips down to the Selçuk's bathroom."

It meant that this was the way the world was: a place where iron, nickel, and other heavy elements collapse in towards the center, get pulled into the dense nucleus; light elements like oxygen and potassium come to the surface, and women sit on their toilets washing their mothers.

Cemil looked to see what the old woman's reaction would be to what Mrs. Nermin had said. The woman fixed her bleary eyes on Cemil. Her face gave no indication that she was listening or had heard any of the things said by those who'd spoken.

Cemil put the aluminum strips back in their place. "I'll go up and take a look. I still don't get where this water is coming from!" he said.

The women exited through the bathroom door and headed towards the entryway. The old woman stood there in the doorway of her own room. She reached out as Cemil was following the other women out and weakly clasped his wrist, asking: "will you help me solve the murder?"

10

Cemil and Nazlı didn't have much of a relationship with their neighbors. On the floor above them there was a couple who looked young from far away but got old when you saw them up close. The woman was really skinny, the man was tall and well-built. They both displayed an exaggerated desire to look young: The woman wore jeans tucked into leather boots and a leather jacket with tassels, the man wore sleeveless white t-shirts and washed his car every day. They both dyed their hair. On some nights the man would drive his car around the apartment complex. There was something off about this man: the car moved extremely slowly, and there would be purple lights lit up on the inside. Cemil wasn't sure if living in a one-bedroom apartment was also part of their desire to remain young, since the couple had two daughters and three grandchildren. Even though they only came once in a while, whenever the children did visit they couldn't fit in the house. The man would stand outside his doors with his son-in-laws, smoking cigarettes.

The apartment below them was similar; the tenants often changed. Before the woman had come to tell him that his bathroom was leaking, Cemil already knew a few things about the people who lived in the apartment downstairs.

They had moved in a few months ago. They were quieter than the former tenants (two noisy female students): there was a man who was more or less middle-aged, who would sometimes snap loudly at his mother: "Mom why are you acting like that!" and then there would be the clanging of a chain as it was dragged against the radiator pipe. Then sometimes the man called from outside: "Did you give her the medications?" and a young woman answered from the downstairs window: "okay, okay!"

27   BARIŞ BIÇAKÇI

In the daytime, whenever he heard these sounds he would see three things: first, a fat young woman looking out from the window of the downstairs apartment on the side of the building where the entrance was, along with an old woman with white hair. The fat woman standing up on her feet, the old woman sitting, her head only partially visible from the lower right corner of the glass. The second were diapers, wet naps and medicine boxes inside of semi-transparent blue garbage bags left by the door of the downstairs apartment. The third was a fifty-year old man with glasses who walked his cute long-eared dog around the parking lots surrounding the business center. One day this man had even gone up the wrong floor and knocked on their door, surprising Cemil when he saw him.

Putting all of these things together, Cemil figured out that there was an old woman living downstairs with her attendant, and that the woman's son and his wife either lived in the apartment complex or somewhere else nearby. Most of the time, the man brought his dog when he came to look after his mother. And because it probably bothered her, the dog's leash would be tied to the radiator pipe. The dog never barked or growled but continuously tugged at the chain, clearly trying to move, or reach for something. The sound of the chain clanking on the radiator pipe, and the sound of the man scolding his mother had merged in Cemil's mind, since the man scolded his mother in the same way that he would scold a dog, maybe it wasn't actually the dog tied to the radiator pipe but his mother! If that was true, Cemil would have been delighted. If you thought about the constant tugging on the chain and the clanging sound it made, it meant that the old woman had to be quite energetic. But she wasn't. It was the medications keeping her alive. They were putting her in diapers. They had moved her far away from her home, shut her away in a small apartment with a home nurse. They couldn't live with her, so they came and visited her instead.

Cemil inspected his own bathroom and saw that a thin stream of water was leaking onto the floor from the space where the sink faucets met the wall. He went downstairs to the entrance of the apartment storeroom to shut the valve. He shut it off. Clockwise. It was closed by turning it clockwise. He went upstairs and took off the faucet, wrapped linen around the connector threads. The linen was wrapped around. While working without anyone watching him, he worked with skill and speed. He put the faucet back on, opened the valve, and the leak was stopped. But there were always leaks, like little threads, leaking in from the things we experience, from the books we read, from the films we watch, things always leaking into our brains.

"The living brain has the consistency of custard."

He loved these kinds of comparisons that scientists used to try to influence people.

Custard! We could dig into it with spoons . . .

Cemil was remembering a scene from a film he had seen years ago: the film's only good scene. The protagonist was imagining cutting up his brain in a sink. But it didn't really have to have to be the protagonist, basically anybody with a little bit of brains in their head could imagine doing something like that.

Again, like scientists say, our brains have one hundred billion neurons and these one hundred billion neurons connect to one another at ten thousand connection points by means of chemical fluids. Nice. Fluids are nice, they render the impossible possible, render thought possible . . . But as we age, a section of these neurons die. The chemical fluids decrease, and the brain is no longer a custard, it's more like a stale cookie shedding crumbs. The neurons that have to connect to one another no longer connect. They're broken off. And strange, patchy connections that didn't exist before start to emerge, and the old woman, holding onto Cemil's arm asks: "will you help me solve the murder?"

Cemil started the conversation by saying "my warmest regards, Mrs. Editor." He was trying to be sarcastic, it was the only way to go.

"Mrs. Editor, you know when the ancient Greeks were confronted with beauty, it made them sad. And because they were so good at it, they have passed into the annals of history. We modern humans, however, have become restless, confused, and even sometimes angry; but history will not speak of us.

On this beautiful planet of ours, the thing that makes us restless, confused, and enraged is knowing that our species has become quite fragmented, ugly, and shattered ever since the age of the ancient Greeks. Maybe we don't even want to cure ourselves of this pain, who knows. Modern humans tend to reduce the idea of justice to the threatening idea that 'no bad deed goes unpunished.' Intellectuals have also had their fair share of this tendency; they want to punish others, they're confused and angry. You are right to say that literature cannot be made from crude feelings. We have to remain calm.

But I can't completely agree with your view that aphorisms pose a threat to literature. Due to the nature of our biological deficiencies and political absurdities. I mean because we are forced to live our lives without having access to 'the essence of things,' what's the point of literature if we aren't going to write like we actually do know the essence of things, pretending like we possess this knowledge even if for a few sentences! In order for a person to bear not knowing the meaning of life, or whether somewhere else in the universe there exist lifeforms which resemble our own, or how the satanic processes which drive Capitalism work, they require the ability to hold onto doubt—in both the intellectual and moral sense. Maybe it doesn't mean knowing aphorisms but rather making the effort to know them, or just valuing

BARIŞ BIÇAKÇI

the effort to propose the beginning of one. This much is clear, isn't it: aphorisms act as a modern painkiller. A pain that is never alleviated. A pain that always comes back.

It's quite possible you won't like my novel manuscript filled with aphorisms. You might think that my aphorisms are cheap, and on top of that, that they contradict one another. I hope we can talk about this topic again later. For the moment, suffice it to say I was pushed to write this novel by the belief that 'I have valuable experiences that are worth sharing with others' and that this belief is one of the two ridiculous things that men use to console themselves, and that keep them standing on their feet on the path towards old age. The other ridiculous consolation is 'women still find me attractive.' I find that one truly ridiculous, but also can't completely divorce myself from it."

Cemil was restless and angry because the editor was a beautiful woman.

After returning from Istanbul, he had begun talking to the editor in his mind, sometimes out loud, waving his hand or his arms as he walked around outside the apartment complex every day for an hour. A few birds were naturally startled by this noisy two-legged creature, this being who didn't lift off the ground despite how much it flapped its wings.

During these conversations, Cemil talked to the editor about his understanding of literature, about his own past, and his daily life. During these walks the ghost of an attractive man, a mature author and a contrarian intellectual stalked around the apartment complex; buying the newspaper from the lunch counter, going to the management building and paying the monthly fuel bill, looking for discounted products at the store, buying toilet paper for thirty-two lira. After all, ghosts are just trying to be human, and you get six extra rolls for free.

When Nazlı opened the door, Cemil was gathering up his father's things. His wristwatch, his wallet, his glasses, keys, a small notebook, and the beanie he wore when he slept . . . When he noticed the door opening, he turned around and looked at Nazlı without wiping the tears from his eyes: she was too late.

"I'm sorry!" said Nazlı, confused. Her hand was still on the doorknob. She had noticed that Cemil was crying and was looking at him like she somehow already knew him.

Cemil, hunched over with his father's things in his lap, stood still.

They looked at each other like that for a brief moment. Then suddenly Cemil could picture Nazlı's breasts, swinging happily back and forth, her groaning underneath him. Nazlı regained her composure, asking "is there anything I can help with?" and then while saying "I'm the doctor . . . I mean I'm the intern . . ." she raised her arms a little into the air and with her head bowed looked down at what she was wearing.

Cemil didn't respond. Nazlı took a few steps backwards, exiting the room. The door slowly closed. Cemil started putting his father's things into a navy-blue cloth bag.

It was the middle of March. The weather alternated between bright and overcast and whenever it was clear outside, the room filled with sunlight. Once, Cemil saw his shadow's head laid out on the pillow of his father's empty bed. He didn't know what to make of this game of light and movement. The best thing to do was to stay still; to not disturb his shadow. But a cloud moved into the way and the shadow disappeared. The door opened. Nazlı entered. This time she was wearing a white apron, and had a cup in her hand.

Holding out the cup she said "this will do you some good."

Cemil took the cup without saying anything. After a few sips, he said "my dad is dead! He didn't make it out of surgery . . ."

"I know," Nazlı said, "I asked the floor nurse."

"You're . . ." Cemil said, "you're too late!"

Nazlı motioned for him to sit, and he walked in front of the window, standing with his arms crossed.

"I forced him to get the operation . . ." Cemil said, swallowing his tears.

"My dad was all I had, now he's gone . . . my mother passed away when I was young."

Nazlı put her hand on Cemil's shoulder and asked "Are you an only child? Do you have any other relatives here right now?"

Cemil wiped his nose. He said he had gone downstairs to help a friend with a problem, and then he began to explain his father's illness. Down to the finest detail, as if Nazlı would somehow give him a new diagnosis and prescribe a new treatment. His throat knotted up. He was silent. He felt grateful for Nazlı being there, and for her large breasts. Nazlı helped him gather his things. They exited the room together. The sliding door of the wardrobe as well as the cabinet drawer were both left open, and the two small yogurt cups belonging to Cemil and his father, put out on the windowsill so that they wouldn't go bad, continued to sit there.

The black horse from my childhood wants to run off in every direc-
tion," Cemil wrote, "he wants to bury his head in some hay."

The letter Cemil had written to Nazlı twenty years ago from a shack in Tokat was long and literary like the other letters he wrote in those years. But it was literary like the pleas of a prisoner shut away in a jail cell are literary: all of the details made to rear up on their hind legs, spurred on by the whip of deprivation and longing. And so spiderwebs became important, shadows on the wall, and even the changes in color. In order to survive, to believe secretly in freedom and immortality, you had to notice details and be able to translate them onto paper.

In this letter, Cemil spoke about the trees, about the dark and silent trees in the forest, about their trunks. "There are drawings, designs, even images in these trunks. If fortune tellers looked at them who knows what they would see, convergences and separations." He explained how a snake was slithering from the bottom of a thicket towards a stream. "A translation of Baudelaire by Orhan Veli: *And the caresses of a snake / That crawls around a grave.*" He spoke of the small streams fed by melting snow: he wanted to name each one of them after Nazlı. "I can't think because they flow delicately like your name, they make a soft babbling sound as they run off with my mind." He spoke about clouds: "They puff up with the blue of the sky as though their older brothers are there behind them ready to protect them." Even the bird that tried to smash the shell of a snail with a rock in its beak made its way into this letter.

He tried every trick used by well-read men trying to impress their lovers: As a man in love, he wanted to understand the universe all at once; he dared to grasp at its meaning, while at the same time making sure he didn't brazenly neglect what was right there in front of him. He told the stories of the workers coming from the surrounding villages, recounting each one of their nicknames for each other, praising the flavour of the barley soup with yogurt that they ate in the morning, giving the recipe. He looked at everything with curiosity and wonder, connecting this sense of newness to his love for Nazlı. At the end of the letter he said a few words about what nature made him feel, and was struck by wonder once again:

> "It's so strange that words don't exist in nature! Words are so natural here . . . In the morning looking at the forest, appearing and disappearing behind the low-lying clouds, I feel like Oktay Rifat having just typed up a beautiful poem. When I light up my cigarette I feel calm. As I comb my hair back cheep cheep cheetalinya."

Twenty years ago, Nazlı had written on the last page in pencil:

> "Under the pretense of work, you went looking for words. You love words, sometimes more than people. Pouring out the tea at the bottom of the cup onto the grass, emptying the gutters of rainwater. You'll find them when a memory comes to you suddenly, your eyes bloodshot—the words, I mean. You'll want to touch them, you'll want to fill your pockets with them. Maybe you'll want to push them into a corner with a spoon, squish them and rub them, inhale them. Now I'm going to get undressed and lie face down on our bed. The trees turn, and our house, and the world."

Cemil had laid out a few newspapers on the inside of the aluminum strips in the bathroom ceiling. He wanted to prevent the drops of water from dripping directly from the bathroom upstairs onto the toilet in their own bathroom. He saw that the water drops were pooling on top of the aluminum strips, and when the strips could no longer take the weight of the water they would bow sideways and pour water into the bathroom. Because of this, it wasn't a bad idea to lay down some newspaper, even if Nazlı said it looked bad. Once he heard the sound of water on the newspaper, Cemil would be able to take the necessary precautions, and if he didn't hear any sounds he could still judge the situation by looking to see if the newspaper was wet or not. Whenever they took a bath or flushed the toilet upstairs, he went to the bathroom and looked and listened for the sound of dripping on the newspapers.

When the inevitable did happen and the bathtub leaked and got the newspaper wet, Cemil gathered up the pages and replaced them with new ones. And so, at different times there would be different people looking down at the toilet bowl from in between the aluminum strips on the ceiling: members of the national security council sitting around a meeting table. The city manager opened four-foot bridges all at the same time. A writer who was giving an interview for the first time, getting her photograph taken, who was said to make "quiet literature" but whose greatest skill was most likely not being seen in public . . . and each one of these faces looked down at the toilet bowl with a faint sense of fear and dizziness, knowing it was the spot where one day they would quickly be flushed out of this life.

Cemil sometimes heard conversations during the daytime. There was a knocking at the doors, "your bathroom is leaking!" the neighbors would say to each other. And Cemil too. A few times when he saw that the newspapers on the ceiling had gotten soaked and the water was still dripping, he went and knocked on the upstairs apartment door, "your bathroom is leaking!" That was the password. The password that let you know that the people living in the apartment complex were at war. But it was also a password that made it clear that they were on the same side of a war, and that they shared the same fate.

There was a knock at the door. Cemil opened it without looking through the peep-hole.

"My parents live on the floor below," said the person at the door. A thin, pale-faced twenty-year-old kid. He had slippers on.

"The password?" Cemil asked.

The kid looked without understanding.

"Aren't you going to say the password?"

"The password?"

Cemil asked, angrily, "is our bathroom leaking again?"

"Bathroom? No . . . I was just coming to ask if you had *The Soda Tree*. The one by Sabahattin Kudret Aksal. As he said this, Cemil looked over his left shoulder and pointed at the bookcase with his chin.

"I must have it . . . let's look . . . it's gotta be... "Cemil turned towards the bookcase. He was puzzled.

As the kid watched Cemil search for the book on his bookcase, he stretched his head in past the doorway "We, I mean my mom has seen your books . . . my parents' caretaker is in high school, they gave her homework. They're going to be reading *The Soda Tree*."

Homework?

Cemil found the book. He had bought it years ago from a store selling cheap books. He had only read a few of the stories. He handed the book to the kid. Then he thought he should say something. *"He doesn't speak, he knows that speaking is against nature,"* he said.

The kid looked at him, confused.

"A verse by Sabahattin Kudret Aksal . . . I actually really like Aksal's poetry. I don't really like his stories. It's been a long time since I've read them. I can't say I remember it."

The kid smiled, listening to Cemil, and was probably a little frightened. He said thank you a few times, said he would return the book as soon as the assignment was done, and went down the stairs.

The world is so strange. You expect the person knocking at your door to be the neighbor complaining, but instead it's someone asking for a book.

Three days later the kid came back. This time he had a folder in his hand. "Hey," he called out to Cemil. "I also write a little. Could I ask, would you take a look, read it and tell me what you think?"

Cemil said "of course I'll read it" but couldn't figure out why he had just sounded so enthusiastic. Then, to make it seem more like an obligation, he said "I'll read it."

The kid was very pleased. "Thanks in advance. These are just some of my scribblings. Actually, it's some private stuff. Do they amount to anything? I wanted you to see," he said, as if he had to convince himself as well as Cemil that he was a good person, someone who kept their word. "Thanks again for *The Soda Tree*. I'll bring it back once I'm done," he said, disappearing down the stairs.

Cemil shut the door. For some reason, the kid's phrase "I wanted you to see" had bugged him. He lay down on the couch in the living room and looked at the folder. It had been written on a computer. Perched on the top hand corner of every page was the writer's name: Berkan Gönen.

16

When everything in life has lost its meaning it's only fair, for the sake of consistency, that the *La Liga* and *Bundesliga* matches on tv would stop making sense too. Cemil thought it was absurd that people couldn't ever use their hands, only their feet. The great care that number nine showed for his hair was absurd. It was absurd that after each play, the players and the coaches would look out of the corner of their eyes at the giant screens in the stadium to see if the camera was showing them or not. Cemil shouted "don't do that! Don't do that!" because the only way to fight against the meaninglessness was by narrating the match like an announcer at a wrestling tournament. One nail drives out another.

As he read Berkan's writing, the feeling that "everything was meaningless" came creeping in. When a kid writes, it is nothing more than them trying to show off their sensitivity, wordplay, and scraps of philosophy. Once or twice while he was reading, Cemil shouted out "don't do that! Don't do that!" But he wasn't acting like the wrestling announcer just because the writing was bad. There was a time when I was just as excited and enthusiastic as this kid, he thought. I struggled to squeeze the water out of words, but now it's nothing but academic knowledge and awkward experiences . . .

"Today the grandson of the lady downstairs came by again . . . That Berkan kid. The one who wanted to borrow *The Soda Tree* . . . he's written a few things, he wanted me to read them," Cemil said.

Nazlı was surprised, "you two are that close?"

As Cemil's eyes followed a moth around the living room, he said "no, of course not . . . Everything is meaningless! Life is nothing more than just gigantic molecules making copies of themselves. That which we call life is nothing more than chemistry. All we have to do is memorize the periodic table. That the two most common elements in the universe, hydrogen and helium, are also the lightest elements explains everything you need to know. What are you searching for in a universe that is so light? Meaning is heavy . . . it sinks to the bottom. That's why fortune tellers look at coffee grounds."

For a moment, Nazlı was annoyed at Cemil for being able to spend his days at home just like he wanted, crafting elaborate sentences to complain about the meaninglessness of life. But then she realized exactly why he was talking about it. Her dearest Cemil was actually talking about the passing of time. Nazlı was also interested in the passing of time. She stared at the moth perched on the curtains, its wings folded closed, and it put her at ease. Believing in the days of the week, and thinking about how much of her life she had already lived, yes, everything was meaningless, first the moth would fly around a little, but then it would be reunited with God's mercy. The days of paganism were over.

"What does he write, poetry?" Nazlı asked, "what did you think of it?"

Cemil said that Berkan had tried poetry along with every other genre of literature, and that it was all bad. He read out a few examples.

"I wrote stuff like this when I was young, really rough stuff. But the problem isn't that he's writing bad stuff. Nazlı, I see so much confusion in this kid's writing . . . the confusion of someone who wants to do something, who feels like they have the ability inside, but who doesn't know what to do with it. Should I stay or should I go? The confusion of not having an answer to that basic question. I know it quite well. I'm that way too."

"But," Nazlı said, "not knowing whether to stay or to go, isn't that something all young people wonder! Old people know what they want."

"Ah!" Cemil said, "that's both frightening and beautiful." Then he looked at the books, the set of music on the bookshelf, and the CDs with their colorful spines. Was he looking at things he had wanted and then obtained, or was he hoping that by looking at them, he would know what it was he wanted?

What was it he had wanted when he was a student in college and couldn't find a copy of *Beyond the Squat Minaret,* and had spent two days in a row going and reading it at the National Library? He had read those long, uniformly arranged stories in that room with the high ceiling and the floor covered with brown carpet. Sunlight coming in from the narrow window and falling right onto the book. Six stories in two days. On the second day when he returned to read the remaining stories, for that one moment he knew what he wanted: to be one of Yusuf Atılgan's characters.

In the first year he was married to Nazlı, on that snowy Monday when he had bought an etymology dictionary, a vernacular dictionary, and an Ottoman dictionary, he knew what he wanted. He had gone to work until Monday afternoon, got out and bought the dictionaries, walked with them through the crowd of people on Selanik Caddesi, and thought that the things he had in his hands were heavy but elegant tools for meaning and explanation. He wanted to deepen his relationship to words, to widen the path of expressions. When he got home, Nazlı was in the kitchen, and the apartment smelled like yellow soap. During those years, good smells always brought so many things to mind. It was a more meaningful life then, full of good smells.

While looking at the bookcase, Cemil explained the conclusions he'd made to Nazlı: "One: deprivation and longing keep us sharp, keep us outside the bounds of time. Two: fulfilling desire turns us into Jell-O, throws us back into time."

17

In Germany, at the edge of the Black Forest, in a city with stone bridges and buildings with pitched roofs and a river running through them, there lived a philosopher who leaned his back against the hundred-year-old trees and wore pressed velvet, who drank aged wine in darkened silver chalices and who once said that his was the age in which man had materialized.

Cemil, on the other hand, lived in an apartment complex. He was not living the kind of life in which a person could feel their own deeply grounded relationship with time. Instead, like everyone else in the petit-bourgeoisie, he just made a big deal about the fact that it was passing. Even though he really loved clocks as objects, he did not at all like wearing one on his wrist.

One day while heading to an indoor soccer match, before the bus had exited the first stage of the complex, an old man got on and sat in the chair in front of him. There were very few people who left the apartment complex in the evening to go into the city, so the bus was empty. He was an adorable little man, but he looked restless. He was looking at his watch. Is he trying to get someplace, Cemil wondered. As the bus left the part of town filled with apartment complexes, and took the road that went towards the front gate of the sugar factory, the man turned and asked "do you have a watch?" Cemil showed his forearms and said "unfortunately no!" Cemil thought it was strange that the man would be asking for the time since he had his own wrist watch. But then again, there must be a reason, he thought. Perhaps the man is conducting some research about the theory of special relativity! When the bus got on the Istanbul Highway, the man grew even more restless and adorable. Cemil went to pull his bus card out of his wallet. The machine had printed the time when he had boarded the bus next to his remaining balance on the card. He could say that they could use it to get a close approximation of the time. At that moment, the old man extended his arm with the watch on it towards Cemil and said "I have a watch actually, and it works. But my granddaughters, naughty girls, sometimes when I'm sleeping they mess with it, they set it forward or back, and I don't notice. I'm always doubting what time it really is. Are they up to no good again, I'm always asking myself. I feel the need to double check. That's why I asked." Cemil liked how the man smiled at this, how he explained it in a cheerful way. Cemil looked at the old man laughing at himself as he looked out the window. Even when we escape being a plaything in the hands of time, we end up being playthings in the hands of the young.

It was only about a week after this incident when the table clock in the house stopped working. The clock was at least fifty years old. Sitting on the coffee table, Cemil remembered when he could only see it if he stretched out his neck. Back when his mother was still alive. When his mother was alive, his father was alive, and the clock was new and round, very beautifully round.

Now it was broken; its stem wasn't turning. The spring might be broken. Constantly spinning your head around is tiring work, as much for metal as for humans. Making people certain that it was ten to four could have paved the way to breaking the spring. Because having to be certain is tiring too.

Before going out for his walk, he put the table clock in a small plastic bag and took it with him.

It made him sad to be taking the clock out of the house. It was the feeling that he was doing something wrong . . . He went up to the second floor of the business center with the plastic bag in his hand. He went into the repairman's shop with its window display showing off wrist watches, battery-operated table clocks, and a bunch of large and small batteries inside of colorful packages. The shop was tiny, taking one step inside from the door brought you face to face with a tall countertop made of thick glass. The small screwdrivers, pincers, tweezers, and magnifiers were reassuring. The repairman's head was leaned forward, deep in his work, his arms out of sight. When Cemil saw the man so engrossed in his own work, he felt as though his sadness had passed for a moment. But when the repairman lifted his head up, showing his face, Cemil felt the deep sense that he was doing something wrong. The man had a goatee, and Cemil immediately didn't trust him. If you can't trust a clock repairman in this world, then who can you trust! Standing in front of a tall counter led to a feeling of subordination resembling nausea. He took a deep breath, fished the clock out of the bag and showed it to the man, explaining the problem.

For one moment, Cemil thought that the clock repairman was going to ask him "why me?" in the innocent tone of a young girl to whom he had just pronounced his love.

"It will be ready about this time tomorrow," the repairman said.

That day, as Cemil took his walk around the first section of the apartment complex, he was limping. He didn't look up and take in the view of Etimesgut, or see the open grounds of the sugar factory, or the train tracks that were visible from the road he was walking on. The clown standing in front of the newly opened clothing store pulled his red and yellow striped socks up towards his knees. A military cargo airplane, flying so low it looked like it was going to crash, passed loudly over the apartment complex. The clock was broken, but life and the sky's blue face continued turning. Peh!

In the evening, just before Nazlı got home, he cooked spaghetti. They ate a walnut, cheese, and carrot salad together. They drank tea, they ate pumpkin seeds. As Cemil listened to Simply Red's album *A New Flame*, he got even sadder. The album was at least twenty years old, it wasn't made up of sounds, it was a collection of memories. And the center of things had changed. It wasn't at home anymore, but at a clock repairman's shop . . .

Nazlı thought that Cemil's sadness had to do with his book. "Any news from the publisher?" she asked.

"No!" said Cemil. "No, I'm waiting. But in the meantime, I keep having these conversations by myself with the editor."

"How come? The editor's probably pretty, isn't she."

"Yes," Cemil said, and then something broke inside of Nazlı, and inside of Cemil. They gazed at each other.

"Does it bother you that I asked?"

"I'm anxious because the clock isn't here at home."

"Oh Cemil!" Nazlı said, responding to him, "what doesn't make you anxious?!"

The next day, when Cemil went to get his clock from the repair shop, he saw that the door was closed. He looked in through the glass door. The parts of the clock lay scattered all over the counter. The bell on the top had been removed, the dial had been taken out from the glass housing, and the metal frame, and the spokes, tongs, tumblers, tie-down buttons, small and large screws and nuts, sat in pieces on the counter. Cemil looked on at this scene while holding his breath as if staring at the inner organs of a living thing: is there any sign of life? Something moving? A pulse? His ears were humming. He paced in front of the store, and asked about the repairman in the stores next door. "He'll be right back," they said. He turned and stopped on the second floor of the business center, and watched the people filling out betting coupons on the entrance floor in front of the dried nuts and fruit seller. The repairman was nowhere to be seen. He had decided to go home, but as he exited the business center he spotted the repairman.

Trying to be calm, he said "I came by for the clock."

The repairman said "it will be ready this evening."

Cemil said "the clock is quite precious to me, one of my most intimate possessions! A timepiece is quite a private thing. You of all people should be able to grasp that fact. It's . . . the clock . . . how could you just leave it lying there like that on the counter!" Then he exited. He thought that speaking to a watch expert made it necessary to use outdated words.

"I didn't have what I needed, I went to go get a new spring from Ulus," the repairman answered, showing the little black plastic bag he had in his hands.

Cemil shook his head in dissatisfaction. He said he would come back that evening. People just couldn't be convinced when it came to the subject of time.

At home, sitting in his chair waiting for evening to come around, he drank a few beers and realized that what he had seen on the watch repairman's counter were in fact his own internal organs. Yes, what had been spread out all over the counter in pieces was nothing other than Cemil himself.

That is the kind of philosophy someone living in an apartment complex comes up with. Three grams worth. For use as medication.

18

When people are young, they want things that can't happen. The mid-afternoon call to prayer rings out on the mosque's broken speakers. A dog barks on and on. A cat smells another cat's ass. Things that can't happen don't.

After reading Berkan's writings, Cemil waited a few days for him to come by. When he didn't, Cemil went downstairs on a day when he couldn't hear the sound of chains rattling against a radiator, and he rang the bell to the apartment. The home nurse answered. Behind her in the living room was the old woman, wrapped up in white and lying on the bed like a sheet of paper. She lifted her head up slightly to look. Cemil said hello.

"I was looking for Berkan . . ."

The nurse said "Berkan is not here. He doesn't live here. He comes by once in a while." She looked back towards the living room, "to see his parents . . ."

I know, Cemil said to himself, about the old woman and the dog chained to a radiator that both live here. A depressing headcount.

"When he comes to visit, if it would be possible for him to stop by, upstairs, that'd be nice," Cemil said. As he turned to go, the old woman tried to get his attention with a move of her hand. The nurse looked at Cemil, not understanding why he wasn't leaving. Cemil motioned with his eyebrows. As both of them looked at the old woman, she made a signal again for him to come closer. Cemil couldn't resist, he took a small step forward. The nurse moved aside, and he took off his shoes and entered the apartment, then approached the woman. She grasped Cemil by the arm with her tiny hand and asked "will you help me solve the murder?"

Cemil looked at his arm, which he had extended towards her slightly, to make it easier to hold onto. He had goosebumps.

The next day Berkan came by. Cemil felt anxious. The kid looked at him like he was going to read his fortune. He waited excitedly to hear what was going to be said. With the folder in his hand, Cemil tried to think of a few things to say, maybe he could say he saw a road, or some things that had increased, marriage, that he saw money, then he decided on the conversation he had been having in his head over the last few days. He praised the kid's enthusiasm. How could you write about all of these things any other way? Writing a lot is a good thing. But all of those show-off sentences, those fussy expressions, what was their purpose? The peacock is not a well-loved species of bird in the world of writing. "If it was up to me, I'm partial to sparrows," Cemil said. Berkan was taken aback. "Sparrows?" he asked, confused. "Or they could be pigeons," Cemil said, "what are you reading now?" The kid listed a few fantasy novels, and in the end mentioned Dostoevsky. Then he was quiet. Cemil understood that the kid wasn't very well read. For some reason, he started giving a speech about the use of humor in Dostoevsky. The writer he loved so much mostly used situational comedy in his humor. Some of his characters were downright hilarious. "Whereas Melville and Henry James are writers whose humor feels kind of forced." Berkan looked towards the door, waiting for the bell to ring, or for Cemil to catch his breath. It was clear that he didn't understand what Cemil was saying. But he assumed Cemil must be an important person. His friends must talk about him like "oh man, that guy is crazy, ha!"

This crazy guy moved on to another topic before the bell rang. He took out a copy of *Literary Companions* magazine with a big dark red cover from his bookcase. He talked a little bit about the magazine, which they published back in the late eighties. Then he opened up the magazine to a page and handed it to Berkan. On the page was a letter that Turgut Uyar had written to another magazine about fifty years earlier. Along with some commentary, *Literary Companions* had reprinted the remarkable letter. Berkan struggled his way through it. He gave the issue back to Cemil. Cemil was excited. "Check out this part especially!" he said, this time reading out loud: "the poetry that has survived to this day, in all of its weakness, its scrawniness, is a reflection of the bard's understanding of himself as a lone afflicted soul or, better yet, his memory of the phenomenon. In my opinion, the bard is simply someone who loves poetry and tries to grasp it. And not just in a few special situations. He may have a slight disposition for it, but that's it."

Cemil said "I figure you maybe didn't know the word" and explained the meaning of "affliction" and then thought that the kid would probably never come by again.

But Berkan did come. In fact, he started coming by once or twice a week. Today's youth watch lots of science fiction films and read so many fantasy novels and so they love having a crazy person in their lives; they wait excitedly for new adventures.

Berkan was in his last year in the communications department. They talked about school, about being a student, about his friends, and how the world of work would be waiting for him when he finished school. They drank beer and ate peanuts. The kid had not given up on bringing what he had written to Cemil, on those conversations filled with metaphors, or on listening to the harsh critiques. As time went on, Cemil also took a liking to Berkan. He enjoyed having an influence on the young man and felt genuinely sorry for him. His writing was cheap, bad. And because he was doing it continuously without stopping, his writing was a dusty, cloudy mess. Despite whatever Cemil told him, Berkan saw himself as a writer, and he wanted things that weren't going to happen. Cemil realized he wasn't going to be able to pull him out of that mess. He was going to get lost in it.

Maybe if he starts reading a lot more, Cemil thought, if he reads a lot more, if he becomes more curious . . .

Life is full of coincidences, so full of them that on some days it's possible for a person to run into their own childhood.

When Cemil ran into his twenty-four-year-old self at a small park in Anıttepe, he said "what a coincidence!" and looked at young Cemil's unflabby face, and his curly hair which fell to his forehead, trying to see whether or not he had a weapon in his hand.

Young Cemil did not have a weapon in his hand. He was holding a half-drunk bottle of soda. Cemil could still feel the coolness of the bottle in his fingers.

It was a day in May when the sun was not in the sky but hiding somewhere underneath his feet as he walked. Cemil (the young one) had left his house around noon to see the contemporary English painters exhibit he was interested in seeing after reading about it in a newspaper. He had walked to Kızılay and gone into the exhibit hall in Zafer Market. For Cemil, it was an especially important time for literature, music, and cinema. A film, for instance, could either save your life or cut it short like a careless surgeon: you go down to have your tonsils operated on and get back up with one of your kidneys taken out. Cemil stopped for a second at the top of the stairs going down to Zafer Market. If I can be patient, he thought to himself, but then immediately after that it felt like his head was touched by a magic wand. Like all young people who want something, he didn't know what to believe in. He was wavering between patience and magic. Cemil wanted to write beautiful poetry and beautiful novels. He sincerely believed that small, gradual steps would lead him to his chance of being a good poet, a good writer. But on the other hand, he couldn't avoid imagining that it was all still an impossibly large step to take.

BARIŞ BIÇAKÇI

In the labyrinthine exhibit hall, there were small groups of people moving from one room to another. A young couple was walking hand in hand, kissing in the corners of the exhibit. As Cemil walked into one section he saw them. He was happy to see the girl filled with passion, life was full. He didn't want to interrupt them, so he quickly turned his head towards the painting to his right and stood astonished at its beauty. Cemil was still there looking at the painting as the couple quietly left the room behind him with embarrassed steps. In the painting entitled "Even Dwarfs . . ." he saw a figure with its back turned away from a group of people who were clearly immersed in the hustle of daily life, its face practically coming out of the canvas and staring towards Cemil, towards everyone else looking on, at the spectators of the world. The face of a dwarf. As the dwarf looked out he was crying, as much as a dwarf can cry, his tears already close to the ground. The dwarf was looking out and asking "Do you not love me or is it me who doesn't love you? As I open and close the parentheses of my sad legs while walking, am I walking away from you or are you walking away from me? Cemil? Where to, Cemil?"

Cemil moved away from the painting, and left the exhibit hall. He waited for his breath to return to normal. He could hear the sounds of people inside the market talking, walking and drinking tea along with the sounds coming from within him. Echoing sounds, from somewhere deep down, the sound of an explosion. He went in and out of the booksellers, lined up against the long corridors of the market. He got the feeling, standing there in front of the shelves lined with books, that the doors to a new world were opening. Then he suddenly felt overwhelmed thinking about all of the doors. All the doors that would open if he read each one of those books.

When Cemil went out of the market and into daylight, he was tired and hungry. While eating a simit he walked from Kumrular street towards Anıttepe. He bought a soda from one of the streets opening up onto Gençlik street and sat down in a park right next to the store.

While looking to see if young Cemil had a weapon in his hands, Cemil
couldn't stop thinking about those lines from the introduction to René
Char's *Selected Poetry*: "At forty, we die from the bullet that got lodged
in our hearts when we were twenty."

That is to say, whenever you read a sentence like that and it stays
with you, you've already started dying.

There's no need for a weapon.

21

The first option: young Cemil was patiently waiting to become a writer and hoping that he'd grow and mature. He was on his way to find the Great Writer beyond the desert.

He walked for several days under the fierce desert sun, falling down exhausted from hunger and thirst. He tucked himself under the shadow of some cacti, sucking at the roots of the desert plants. Many dangers jumped out at him. The desert was a sinister place. The endlessness clouded his mind, the sun swallowed up everything. A vision he saw while walking enchanted him. When he came to his senses, he was still captivated by the gleaming bangle worn by a stark-naked woman sinking into the water. He closed his eyes with his hands so that he wouldn't lose sight of the woman, then sat down and began to cry loudly. Thinking to himself that he no longer wanted to make it across the desert, he saw the Great Writer's house out between the waving poplars. He knocked on the door. Nobody was home. He remembered that great writers go on walks, that they find new meanings for the stones and plants. He waited until evening. When the sky got dark, the Great Writer showed up with a dry leaf in his hand. "I was also waiting for you!" he said as he ushered Cemil into his home. Writers know everything, or perhaps act like it in front of everyone. He tied a string to the stem of the dry leaf and hung it from the ceiling. He turned to Cemil and asked "How is it?" obviously pleased with himself. He wasn't interested in Cemil's response. "That means you want to be a writer," he said without showing interest. "Look, it's important to cross the desert, but I noticed that you crossed the desert as yourself. If you want to be a writer, you have to cross the desert as someone else. Do you get it? Cross it as a woman for example. Cross it as a tree, cross it as a dog."

Cemil looked with questioning eyes. The sand sticking to his cracked lips was preventing him from speaking. The writer pointed at the desert stretching outside the window with his hand. Cemil set out on his path once again. He had a sense of why he had to cross the desert as something else, but he didn't know how he would do it. He crossed the desert several times. He saw many things, had many experiences. But there was no change. One day the Great Writer said "do you know the secret to the art of writing? It's writing as though you are aware of nothing, not of your observations, the details you notice, nothing. The time has come." He pointed at the table. "Sit and write!"

Cemil sat down, and began writing with surprising ease. He distorted the shapes he remembered from his childhood and from times gone by and turned them into an elegant image, a framed image, and compared it to a journey into the desert. Without even reading it, The Great Writer tore up what he had written. "When a blind person regains their vision, do you know what happens? They believe everything they see!" he said. "Keep writing." Cemil kept on writing, and the Writer kept ripping up what he wrote. Inside the house, words broke free from their sentences, written on torn pieces of paper, and began to fly around. Sometimes under his feet, sometimes in his bed, Cemil would find these words, these butterflies, these flies. Yes, flies. Because sometimes he didn't like them. One day the Great Writer asked "have you read my books?" Cemil said, "of course I've read them. I've read all of them. That's why I came here."

The Great Writer said, "then read them again!" Cemil read them again, and this time they had a totally different flavor. At this point the Writer said, "reread all of the books you've ever read!" It went on like this for years. The Writer aged considerably. One day he confided in Cemil. "I have worried about repeating myself ever since I was young, but then I realized that this was necessary." It was clear from him saying this that he was waiting for Cemil's approval. Cemil understood that the time had come for him to start writing in the style of the Great Writer.

BARIŞ BIÇAKÇI

He took the pen in his hand, and wrote just one sentence. Nothing else came out:

"Writing: imagining that your sense of confusion will sort itself out bit by bit, time after time, and that this time it will somehow come together in perfect order, and that life will merge into some unified meaning."

22

The second choice: young Cemil becomes a writer with a magic touch. Sitting down right away, he writes a seamless novel about the country's recent history.

The novel about a left-wing family with three children begins on the 12th of September 1980, and tells their story over the next twelve years. It begins with these sentences: "When the tanks began slowly moving forward in the middle of the night to take the major roads, the birds in the farthest parts of the forest began shrieking and flying into the air. There was danger. There was danger. At that moment, some of us began running from the narrow streets, from the backyard gardens, from the base of the walls. Two meandering lines running in the darkness. To get the news to our friends. To hide things. Because the city is a forest. The city is a forest. The tanks' gun barrels were a giant eye scanning the streets. We look out from the window. My mother watches from the window. My father is sitting in prison. My father is sitting in prison. When it's my turn, I stand up. My mother is a switchboard operator, I say, my father is in prison. The class laughs. I laugh too. That's the way the world is. The teacher writes on the board: Every evening I share the profits, *kâr*, with my business partner. 'What happens when we don't put a hat over the 'a' in *kar*? The whole class laughs.[1] That's the way the world is. There are soldiers under hats."

The book is told from the perspective of the youngest child in the family. The father is arrested when the coup starts, and they sentence him to death. He remains in prison for nine years. One of the most

---

[1] In Turkish, 'kârım' means 'my profits' whereas 'karım' means 'my wife'

moving chapters in the book is when the son sees his father in the Mamak barracks, in a gym turned into a courtroom. Cemil starts the scene with the body search at the barracks gate, without skipping a single detail. The child sits in a section set apart for observers in the gym, and gets a chill when he looks at the row of empty chairs facing away from him. Then, dozens of detainees dressed in matching pale blue outfits enter the gym in single file. Even though the mother points him out, the child cannot find his father in the crowd. With their heads shaved, with thick-rimmed glasses, they all look alike. Men with their backs turned. When the trial begins, the detainees turn their heads around from where they are sitting to get a look at the audience. In order to see their families if only for a few seconds. But they are immediately stopped by the soldiers. Those who want more than those brief moments take the chance of asking permission to go to the bathroom, getting to see the faces of the spectators as they come back into the gym and sit back down. The child's father does the same thing, giving a great big smile as he comes back from the bathroom. Smiling back at him, the mother shakes her head in response. The child sits frozen. Cemil planned this scene to be the turning point of the novel. The child feels a great sense of regret at staying frozen at that moment, and his life afterwards would always ache from that slender wound. The novel moves between large developments and small events, showing the similarities between the child's psyche and the dominant ethos of the country in the eighties. In the last chapter, the father gets out of jail after nine years. Until this chapter, Cemil would have used an epic, impassioned narrative approach, singing the praises of resistance, but then all of a sudden he changes his tone. He describes the family members of detainees who hear about their sentences being commuted. They come in cars and minibuses from different cities around the country and wait in front of the prison doors, breaking out into a group halay ring dance "in spontaneous joy" while they wait. The excitement climaxes before the prison door opens, and the prisoners are frustrated when they are taken to the military station before being released. Then there are the final embraces, the crying, the shedding of tears, and a lasting terrible sense of resentment. At the end of the novel, the narrator has become a young man and he recalls the night, nine years earlier, when his father was taken into custody. The novel ends with these sentences:

"When the soldiers came for my father, they carefully examined the sewing patterns in my mother's copies of *Burda* magazine as if they were a secret blueprint. They tore them into little pieces when they couldn't figure out what they were. The soldiers knew very few things, they were afraid of the things they didn't know, they wanted to destroy them. We knew many more things than the soldiers did. We wanted the world as we knew it to collapse as soon as possible."

23

The trees sway in the wind; a cloud resembles something and then it doesn't; life is so cruel when a horse slips and falls on the asphalt. And the days go by.

Days passed. Spring had long since arrived. Swifts appeared in the sky. No news came from the publisher. Cemil continued his conversations with the editor.

"Ms. Editor, I am waiting for news from you. It's been two months. Every telephone call excites me: There's news! Things that used to annoy me for being a waste of time now help ease the pain of waiting, and make time pass more quickly, and so I like them. Think about it, I spend hours downstairs with the neighbor's grandson. I listen to him, I read his writing and I talk at him. Days go by like this. News will come!

Ms. Editor, I know you're going to reject my manuscript. Your boss will call and say 'believe me we've never had such a hard time making a decision! You've put us in a very tricky spot Mr. Cemal, you split the publishing board down the middle!' I won't remind him that my name is Cemil not Cemal, and instead I'll apologize for splitting the publishing board down the middle. I will go along with the courteous show put on by your boss. Why pass up the opportunity to be a good person, and to apologize even when there is no need!

I don't want to just put on a show for you. Let's be frank. I am certain that if you all don't publish my manuscript, literature will not have missed out on a single thing. But if you do, you'll have set free one of those literary protagonists created by writers for unreasonable purposes. One more literary creation whose increasing numbers threaten to overrun our world. You and your publishers will have, by your own doing, let them loose onto the sidewalks of the housing complexes where you and your publishers live. That is why some things should stay in books. I'm talking about one of those 'failed writer' characters from short stories and novels that writers love so much. Literary history is full of these types. It's clear why they like them so much, right? Writers can walk around in peace knowing that even if they don't have the emotional depth needed to write normal characters, they can still use the unsuccessful writers living deep inside of them. What's more, when they invent characters who are trying to write, or are writing but can't get what they write published, they are able to say things that are hard to say by talking about the details from their own books. They have the luxury to say things that will be exempt from criticism. In fact, some writers give over the pen to their characters completely, and when we come to the end of the book we suddenly realize that we were reading the book that the character wasn't able to get published!

It's true. Writers whose books don't get published make for good protagonists in novels. It's also that I am a masterful chess player and have a special interest in paleontology.

However, Ms. Editor, I have wanted to be a poet, a writer, since my childhood. There are two reasons for this. One is the memory of when we visited my father's poet friend when I was a child. The poet's way of speaking, his dress, his house overlooking Botanik Park, his work room with paintings on the wall and books everywhere . . . I was enchanted. The truth of this memory, like many others, was distorted by fantasy. We humans don't really have much use for pure reality. Reality is for animals of prey. Fish, for example, know what is true and what is a lie since it's required to stay alive. Deer are like that too. Anyways, whether it was true or not, the memory was magical. I wanted the enchantment to last. We all want enchantment to last.

The second reason why I want to be a poet and a writer is also from my childhood. My father would constantly explain things to me that were full of pain, grief, and distress. We lost my mom when I was

BARIŞ BIÇAKÇI

still six years old. The poor man, he thought the best way to deal with a motherless child was to have him grow up quickly. He would bathe me in the waters of his own pain. I began to perceive my father's convoluted world as my own. We have soft skulls as children. When I was with my friends at school, or among the people in the street, I heard my father's long and mournful sentences in my head, and they became like a beam I was walking across. They called me an acrobat, they called me a jester, they said I would be a writer. For most people these are all the same thing. The thought of this put me at ease: I was navigating between people and the world's pain by running on top of a long beam. Whether as a writer, or as a jester, it didn't matter.

You also think about how nice it is knowing that there are things worth explaining, that one day you will explain them, that you will write them down. But once you've had this thought, it sure can make a person miserable! The highest position in this world is that of those in the literate class. But even that starts to not be enough for you. Being a human starts to not be enough for you. You want to be a world.

I started with poetry. Inside me, deep down, I felt that there was an enclosed space where there were no words, where meaning flew around banging into things like a bat. I imagined that I would be able to descend into this space with poetry, or at least move down farther towards it with each line. But writing poetry does not mean explaining things that already exist, it means creating something from nothing. Ms. Editor, let me assure you, people who pick up a pen to write poetry longer than three sheets of paper really have to concentrate. In the end, all that's left of someone in the world is their hide and some bone. After struggling for years, I gave up poetry. It wasn't going to happen. Thank God I was mature enough to see that. Once in a while, whenever I pick up my poetry notebook and read the poems I wrote when I was twenty, this is what I see: the bashfulness of a violin player and an obsession with Marlon Brando.

At the same time as I tried to wrestle with poetry, I was imagining writing a novel that Nazlı could lose herself in because I also wanted to include her. Men want to embrace women. Pressing Nazlı's head to my chest, smelling her hair, it's what I long for.

Ms. Editor, when you write, whenever you tell stories, you can embrace a woman and become another person. Respectfully yours . . ."

24

What do we think is worth explaining?

They found a spear in a cave in France they think belonged to someone who lived approximately fifteen thousand years ago. Creating a larger space for the arm allowed for the spear to be thrown farther and with greater strength, and this tool, made from the neckbone of a deer, had a picture of a baby goat defecating on it. Depicted perching on top of the baby goat's poop were two birds. The birds were most likely looking for seeds in the poop.

The first Hittite King Hattusili I, who lived sixteen hundred years before the birth of Christ, gave a long description in his will as to why he had chosen his grandchild rather than his nephew, and then gave the grandson, who was going to assume the throne, some advice: to take care of his health, and to not veer from the words of his elders. "When you have finally grown old," he says, "give yourself a drink and leave the words of your elders aside."

In one of the thousands of poems written by a Chinese poet who lived in the first half of the seventh century after the birth of Christ, he describes the return journey of a man who had to stay away from his family for ten years due to war. He emphasizes the strange un-happiness of this man who should have been happy and excited to rejoin his loved ones: "He could not be pleased returning to his home in good health / even the apple flowers were dropping off, pleased at the coming of spring."

In the journal that Charles Darwin kept on his trip out on the HMS Beagle, he wrote that the natives of Tierra del Fuego were quite enormous, that they obviously shaved their eyebrows and beards with sharp seashells, and that they spoke like they were coughing. In his journal Darwin described how the natives chose to eat old women rather than dogs in times of famine.

In the beginning of the nineteenth century a German officer serving as a staff officer for three years in the Ottoman army described the women of Ramallah as being famous for their beauty, and that carrying weight on top of their heads made it possible for these women's bodies to develop pleasingly.

A professor of agriculture, who knew and loved every square inch of our country, tells us in a book published in 1957 that he wandered for hours after a dark-eyed sheep on a day in May in order to understand which grasses it ate on the steppes of Central Anatolia. A few chapters later he gives a breakdown of the fall colors of a forest in the Central Black Sea region: "Dark green fir, light green pine. Gold-yellow leaves, flickering poplar. Leafy hornbeam leaves. Orange-yellow and red leaves are beech. Rust-colored leaves are oak."

One of the workers on the construction site of the apartment complex describes an old man who runs a teahouse in Horasan to his friends drinking tea during an afternoon break. He says that the old man's tea was tasty and strong, that one time a truck driver who drank it was able to drive as far as Izmir without stopping, and adds "the smell of the tea was something else, those women who have breasts like tangerines, it was just like their smell."

Cemil also talked to Berkan about the mood at universities in the eighties, when it was forbidden to sit in crowded groups in the cafeteria. One day they didn't let him into school (and his home a few days after that) because he had a beard. He told Berkan how an official letter had arrived at his home warning him that a disciplinary investigation would be launched if he continued with similar behavior. "For me, university was the place where I first met İlhan and Metin. Besides these friendships, there isn't anything to say about my time at university that makes it any more interesting than my military service."

BARIŞ BIÇAKÇI

25

In the middle of the poster was written: "AND I DON'T HAVE A KITE IN NOVEMBER!" and right below it, "Poetry Magazine," and at the very bottom it stated the exhibit's location and time. At the top of the poster, drawn in indistinct lines, was the sky. There really weren't any kites up there.

In 1987 there was little value, from an artistic standpoint, in composing a line of poetry starting with the conjunction "and," which then mentioned the word kite and then its absence. But it was valuable inasmuch as it resembled an excited and blundering hello, a hand outstretched and then pulled away in embarrassment, a smile seen from far away. As he entered the exhibit hall of the library, Cemil was greeted with this handmade poster. Thirty pieces of poetry were printed on brown wrapping paper in black ink, hanging from the wall. Looking at the names underneath the poems, he understood that the exhibit was for two different poets.

"Your name isn't on the poster!" Cemil said.

"It's underneath the poems," answered Metin, "The day that we get away with not having to write them down is the day we'll have become true poets!"

Laughing, he looked at his friend standing a slight distance behind him. There was a kind of childish impertinence to their attitude, their small eyes constantly moving around.

"I don't think it's right to mix art and Sufism together," Cemil said.

Metin suddenly got serious, short tempered. "Us either, us either . . ." he said. "İlhan and I have a joke about my signature . . ." he extended his hand, "Let's introduce ourselves! Metin and İlhan." İlhan also extended his hand in an earnest way. He looked more serious compared to his friend. It was clear that he was taking the show seriously.

They introduced themselves. On that day, they told each other their names, as well as the names of many other poets and writers. İlhan and Metin's tastes were basically the same; Cemil liked other things.

Three days later, Cemil helped them pack up the exhibit. That evening, at Metin's student house in the Gazi District, they hung the poems on the wall of the living room. Metin made spaghetti and fried potatoes. They drank Çubuk wine. At one point that night, İlhan said that he could use the twists and turns of poetry so that they resembled a woman's curves; he drew something in the air with his hand, but he looked more like an orchestra conductor than a young womanizer. Metin criticized him for using overly sexist language like he always did. "For me, the wrinkles of poetry are the same as those of the elderly!" he said.

Cemil, drunk, read poems from Oktay Rifat's *Moth Holes*. Then he said "For me, this is poetry!" Metin and İlhan stood up at the same moment and applauded.

They began spending most of their time together. Some nights after drinking beer on Sıhhiye Street, they'd go partway into the train tunnel in front of Sıhhiye bridge, walking on the tracks towards Metin's house. The city lights reflected off the rails. Walking together in the dark, the three friends named these lights that followed them the Ankara Reflection Train. These walks made the trio feel like they were watching a good film. It brought the three of them closer together. They were excited and sincere, but serious. They eagerly shared and discussed their writing with one another. Six months later, this time at a club in Kızılay, the three of them organized a poetry exhibit and lecture together. Very few people came other than the people they knew. They participated in protests organized by the student association, and they read poetry. They wrote a few declarations that didn't use the lingo that was popular with the student movement of the time. Their declarations weren't endorsed, and the three friends were accused of bohemianism. After seeing *Jules and Jim* at a film festival, they spoke to each other in French for a while. After seeing the film *Chaos* by the Taviani Brothers, they got interested in Italian. One day they went to school early, and on the chalkboards they wrote these three sentences of Yusuf Atılgan's story, "The Ticking of the Clocks." "I am thinking about the hyena at the Izmir Fair. The concrete base of its cage is worn down on all sides from walking around it. The worn-down line marks the longest path in the cage." When Cemil's father died, the three of them were there together at the cemetery. When they met Nazlı, İlhan said, "Let's start a three person band, and Nazlı will be our only fan!" Cemil said that that would work out better for them than it did for the theatre group in the Tanpınar story, "A Journey by Train." They came up with a lot of ideas like this. Metin got the idea to kidnap bigwigs from the government and to torture them by reading them from the same book for days on end. They had serious conversations about which book they would read. Cemil suggested *Our Brother in Law in Çamlıca*. İlhan thought *The Sound and the Fury* or *Auto-Da-Fé* would work: "Fuckers need to be taken by surprise!" A few years later when they got jobs, Cemil asked "let's put out a poetry book, what do you say?" Metin and İlhan both said it would be really great.

None of these dreams came to fruition. But what was even more painful was that they all slowly gave up writing and imagining together. And the kite in "And I Don't Have a Kite in November" went from being a childish metaphor for freedom to being one for imagination, giving it its true meaning. Cemil married Nazlı, and they moved to an apartment complex and into a two-person world of imagination. After living in Izmir for twelve years, Metin returned to Ankara and started an engineering company. İlhan married a psychologist and they had a kid.

The city strung up barbed wire along the train tracks and it became impossible to walk on the rails from Sıhhiye to Gazi District. The city lights were still reflected on the train tracks, but the journeys of the Ankara Reflection Train went on alone.

Due to the rotation of the Earth, we are traveling at a speed of about 350 meters per second at our current latitude. The Earth travels around the Sun at about 30 kilometers per second, and the Solar System travels around the Milky Way Galaxy at about 200 kilometers per second. The Milky Way Galaxy spins around the galactic center at 270 kilometers per second while simultaneously moving through space at around 600 kilometers per second.

Life isn't moving forward, Cemil thought. It could very well be falling behind.

27

One day Cemil was coming back from shopping at the market when he saw Berkan's grandmother looking out from the bottom corner of her window. The poor woman seemed to notice Cemil and tried to wave. She raised her hand, and then slowly moved it down to her side. That was all. Then all of a sudden the assistant appeared in the window and lowered the woman's hand. If she hadn't, it would have fallen and broken.

Cemil decided that he would help this old woman with a stomach full of medicine, whose name he didn't even know (he hadn't asked Berkan!), who was lying in a white gown under white sheets, to help her solve the murder. He might not have been a good detective but he was a good person, altruistic.

Cemil's family had done what they could to make sure he wasn't a spoiled child: His mother had died when Cemil was only six, his father saw his son as someone to share in his pain. This large, handsome, but emotionally stunted man wasn't capable of coping with the death of his wife or to be a protective adult able to conceal his feelings around his child. Their roles were reversed. "We're alone now!" his father said, "we've got nobody!" Their loneliness wasn't enough on its own, so the lives of historical figures helped explain their great loneliness. Emperors, commanders, presidents, great artists. Cemil listened quietly to his father's explanations without bursting into tears, storing everything in his memory in high fidelity. He walked around the empty rooms of the emperor's palace while listening to the sounds of his own footsteps. Looking past the endless plains of the commander, he couldn't see anybody. Cemil grew up with the pain of not knowing exactly what things meant. He listened to his father and then to everyone else, always trying to console each one of them.

When he turned twelve, he reprimanded his father for the first time. "If you have to lie, Dad, please lie to yourself!" Middle-aged women couldn't leave this handsome widower alone. He used his son as a shield to guard against women pursuing him, a pursuit which would inevitably lead to deceit.

Cemil didn't have any problems going through adolescence. His voice only sounded deeper when telling the woman on the telephone "my father isn't home, he's out of town!" And the times when his father really wasn't home he'd look forward to his return.

At twenty years old, he was a high-strung, unhappy man. He didn't live according to his own inner voice, but according to those voices coming from outside. When he did listen to this inner voice, he acted strange and childish. Someone even thought he was an actual mad-man. He got married in his thirties, and it was his wife who ended up bearing the weight of real things on her shoulders. But he continued having deep spiritual conflicts and developed a few obsessions. In his forties, he fed his obsessions every day like a pet. When the season for it came, he made jam. And he became a quiet, calm man who tried to help old women.

The purpose behind building the apartment complex was more or less to house people like him. They made connector roads to the Istanbul Highway, set up new bus and minibus lines, and these special public buses began running.

Soon the metro would be coming too.

28

The sugar sparkles as it pours; they leave the strawberries in the sugar overnight.

Strawberry jam: the greatest promise of going back to the beginning.

Before Nazlı went out in the morning, she put the pot on the stove to simmer. Cemil was left at home alone with the jam. The jam began to boil with pink foam. He moved it a little over the stove top. The smell of strawberry jam enveloped the house, lashing everything together. Five times around the house, ten times. It was connecting everything, wrapping it up, taking it hostage: time, calendars, Junes. It didn't let a single memory go. If there was something in the world you could call "the first", if that was still around, then maybe its memory was set free.

The memory of the first time that Nazlı and Cemil had sex.

Cemil had drunk beer with Metin and İlhan at Büyük Express. They had drunk a lot. He thought of Nazlı. He was thinking of her lips and her skin, smooth like water. If you leaned out of a slowly moving boat and dipped your hand into the glittering water, it would be soft, it would embrace you but then toss you back out. That was Nazlı's skin.

Leaving his friends, he went to the Mithatpaşa Post office. He called Nazlı in the middle of the night. "I want to see you!" he said.

"If you want, you can come over," Nazlı whispered. Her roommate Hale was already fast asleep and she didn't want to wake her up.

Cemil wound his way to Nazlı's house. Nazlı opened the door before Cemil could ring it. She took him and led him to the bathroom. She washed her face, wet her head. Then she sat on the edge of the tub and dried her hair. She was wearing a cotton nightgown like a kid would wear. Cemil held onto Nazlı's hips and put his head on her stomach. He couldn't believe how light her nightgown was: could something like this really exist in the mortal world? In order to find out, he lifted his head up and looked at Nazlı's face and then stuck his hands underneath her nightgown. He caressed her legs, he moved upwards, and when he put his hands inside of Nazlı's panties she said "hey!", drawing out the y, drawing it way out. She put Cemil's hands down, and laid his head back down on her stomach as she dried her hair. She took him and led him to her room, they went through the two corridors of the apartment, one short and one long, in silence. The light of Nazlı's lamp shone on her room; you couldn't make out what was furniture and what was shadow. You couldn't make out who was Cemil and who was Nazlı. As Cemil stood there, Nazlı undressed him. She took off his wet shirt, his undershirt, his pants, his socks. She laid him down on the bed. Then she locked the door to the room and smiled as she turned around, embarrassed at what she had just done. Could a smile like this really exist in the mortal world?

"Alright, go to sleep!" Nazlı said, stretching out on Cemil's side although neither one of them believed it. Cemil wanted to cover her up, wanted to take her underneath tables, to the little houses he made in his childhood out of pillows and scarves at the base of the sofa. He wanted to take her inside of the joy of that makeshift house. He wanted to never let her go again. At first they were both afraid. Then Cemil realized that Nazlı was a field of flowers. Together they were pleased with this colorful, gently blowing expanse, and at that moment Cemil said the only thing he knew how to say: "Nazlı!"

After that, twenty-one years after that, without there being the slightest emotional discrepancy between the two moments, he said again, "Nazlı!"

He took a spoonful of jam from the pot and poured it into a porcelain tray. Tilting the tray slightly, he looked at the consistency of the jam. He turned the oven on. He separated the foam from the top of the pot with a spoon. He poured jam into the jars that Nazlı had placed on the counter.

BARIŞ BIÇAKÇI

Three medium sized and two small jars. Cemil closed the lids tightly. The jam looked so nice in the jars, demonstrating once again their moving promise: "It's possible to go back to the beginning: Nazlı and Cemil are waiting on a distant shore in their most youthful and naked state." When Cemil travelled to that distant shore, it wasn't Nazlı and himself that he found, but the realities of life: other young women and young men. New sovereigns over the realm of desire.

The egg cell combines with the sperm cell, bringing one single cell into being. And this cell divides, turning into two cells. Then these two cells divide. Four, eight, sixteen, thirty-two . . . Millions of cells forming a complex, precise organism. Humans are actually nothing other than a number, an inconceivably large number. And when they die, they become a number again. As the cells decay and split up, not a single memory or trace is carried from that complex organism within any of the huge number of atoms which decompose into oxygen, hydrogen, nitrogen, and a bunch of stupid carbon atoms.

Berkan came and said that his grandmother had been admitted to the hospital. The poor woman was in intensive care. Her mind was gone. Her whole body had swollen up. Her intestines had started bleeding.

Cemil realized that he hadn't heard the sound of the chain against the radiator for a few days. He got sad. He invited Berkan in, offered him some apple juice.

It was a hot day in the middle of June. In the afternoon there began the low chatter of the Prime Minister speaking at a parliamentary group. Cemil made breakfast, he scanned the newspaper. He heard the chatter when he sat down on the toilet, taking a popular science book about the formation of the universe with him into the bathroom. Lifting his head, he looked at the ceiling. In the visible part between the aluminum strips there still wasn't anything extraordinary to see, just a prime minister at the lectern . . . but you could hear the menacing sound of large, persistent droplets. It was impossible to read a book about the formation of the universe when the bathroom was leaking. In order to be able to do that, you had to be aware of the essence of things.

Even though they had left early that morning, he knocked on the door upstairs with the hope that they had maybe come back.

He knocked and knocked. Then he listened to the silence of the apartment: it was a ten out of ten in terms of silence, maybe a nine out of ten silence, the silence of air when it whooshes out of post office boxes . . .

He went home. For five to ten minutes, he stared at the prime minister at his lectern: his speech went on inside of a large, dark spot. Drip drip drip.

He tried to read. He listened to music. He couldn't get into it. In the afternoon, he was happy to see Berkan come by unannounced. But of course as soon as he learned about Berkan's grandmother, something settled inside him. He didn't even say that he still wanted to help her solve the murder. Life was moving beyond unimportant things, secondary feelings, as though it were running with all of its strength and speed towards someplace important. You're annoyed that the upstairs bathroom is leaking, then you are sad for an old woman you've seen a few times on her deathbed. After that you get jealous listening to the story Berkan starts telling you, you say "that actually is interesting!" Life isn't going anywhere.

Berkan had fallen in love with a girl and "the interesting thing" was that he had met her on his very first day at the communications department. They were in the same friend group. At first there had been nothing between them. But then one day, "last Tuesday to be exact," Berkan had seen a tiger in his dream. The next day he had explained this dream to her, to Şeyda. Şeyda's eyes had grown wide, she covered her mouth with her hand and, breathing with great difficulty, said that she too had seen a tiger in her dream. "It was running, it was enormous . . ." Berkan had said. "Yes, it was running!" Şeyda had said. "Then all of a sudden it stopped . . ." Berkan had said. "It turned around and looked!" Şeyda had said. "Yes, it turned around and looked!" Berkan had said. "Its eyes . . ." Şeyda had said. "Its eyes . . ." Berkan had said.

They had experienced a mind-bending coincidence, but one which didn't mean anything. So they both fell in love. While listening to Berkan, Cemil also wanted to fall in love. He wanted his mind to be bent by an impractical situation. I need to be in love, he thought. It was strange to think so openly about it, especially verbalizing a need that wasn't connected to any one specific woman. Like being a demanding customer! He was irritated. He was jealous of Berkan, and that's why he listened without giving any reaction to what he was telling him. The kid sat for a little longer and then pensively stood up.

In the evening, Cemil went back upstairs and knocked on the door. A woman with dyed-blonde hair answered. Her face was shriveled, dried out. She looked very unhappy. The way she looked gave no indication she had ever loved or been loved by someone, not even in the distant past. Cemil got angry, but not at the woman of course. "Your bathroom has been leaking all day long. Please don't get water on the floor from now on!" he said. The woman nodded without saying a single thing. She knew as Cemil raised his voice slightly that he was angry at something else completely. He repeated to no one in particular: "From now on not even a single drop of water on the floor! Let's all try to keep things dry! Alright, all together!"

"Alright, sure," said the woman with dyed hair.

30

That night Cemil had a dream. He was at home, someone was ringing the doorbell like they were having trouble ringing it. Maybe they weren't tall enough? Suddenly Cemil thought a tiger was ringing the bell, and he was pleased. "In just a moment, I too am going to see a tiger in my dream. It means I'm going to fall in love." He felt like a young person.

The door opened. Berkan's grandmother was standing across from him; doubled-over. Cemil checked to see if she had an IV in her arm. Poison never completely gets absorbed into the dream, it stays on the surface.

"Will you help me solve the murder?" the old woman asked, still in her hospital gown.

You know how you notice silly little details in a dream? Cemil noticed that the woman was speaking to him using the informal you for the first time. It put him at ease.

"Of course, please, come inside. I was about to say that I would help you," he said, taking the woman to the living room. And since you also worry about silly little things in a dream, it made Cemil anxious that there were no diapers in the apartment. He began talking right away so that the poor woman wouldn't sense his anxiety.

"I think the murderer is a man who cackles like a magpie!" he said, sure of himself. "I can see him in the gutters, on the railing of the balcony. Perching in trees at night. And I bet you he can easily watch everyone from there. That way, planning a murder would be both easy and guaranteed."

The old woman put her hands on her knees. It was customary for women of her age to have giant stone rings on each one of their fingers and bright red lipstick on their lips. She was thinking.

"I get why it's easy, but why is it guaranteed?" she asked.

"Because they're able to laugh like that of course!" Cemil said. "Committing murder and they laugh like a magpie!"

The old woman smiled in satisfaction. "We'll make a good team," she said. "We'll solve all the murders."

"All the murders? Are there other murders?"

"There are!" said the old woman. "Do you know the story of the woman who said that the world rested on the back of an enormous turtle?"

Cemil had just read about it. "you're talking about the woman at the astronomy conference. She got up and criticized the scientists for the absurd things they were saying and then explained her turtle theory."

"Yes . . . well that woman, 'okay so what is the turtle resting on?' she was asked, 'it's turtles all the way down!' she had answered. Now, that answer is important."

"How so? Important in what sense?"

"We are resting on top of a murder and, underneath that, it's murders all the way down," said the old woman. She bent over and started scratching the light brown machine-woven carpet with her ringed fingers, but her fingernails broke off into pieces. "Murders all the way down!" she screamed, "Now wake up!"

Cemil woke up. It was pretty normal for his pillow to be soaked through with sweat whenever he woke up from dreams like this.

31

There was something strange going on with İlhan; Cemil realized it
right away, tried to bring it up. İlhan glossed over it, asked whether or
not he had gotten any news from the publisher.

Cemil spoke with Metin. "Yes," Metin said, "I also noticed. There's
something off with our man recently!"

For a while, İlhan acted like he was taller than he actually was. He
acted like he knew the names of all of the trees and constellations. He
was constantly taking deep greedy breaths, like he didn't want to miss
out on any of the smells brought in by the wind in the summertime. He
was acting like he was the king of books, like he could suddenly tell
you exactly in which book and on which page you could find a beautiful
sentence when it came to mind. He acted like a soloist in a band. Like
he'd directed the film *The Woman in the Window*. Like he'd been the
one who wrote the poem "Sorrow, My Dear or Mint."

"The strangest thing," Metin said, "is that he's acting like he wouldn't
even be mad if he lost playing three-five-eight."

One evening they went to go eat at Net Piknik. İlhan stooped his
head down a little so that he wouldn't hit his head on the first step of
the stairs leading to the terrace. Metin winked at Cemil.

The weather was really hot. They drank beer. They made analogies
about their relationship to that first swig of cold beer. Garlic sea bass
with a big arugula salad. The alcohol mixed in their blood. İlhan said he
was in love. He said it like he was at the end of something that wasn't
ever going to happen.

"We figured as much!" Cemil said. "We knew something was up."

Metin asked who he was in love with.

"Is she in love with you too?" Cemil interjected.

The three of them were excited.

"A girl from work," said İlhan, "Ceren. She started last February. Actually she started earlier but came to our department in February." He couldn't help but laugh for a moment. "We've been seeing each other for a while."

Metin asked a series of questions: "Does she know about Handan? Does she know you have a son?"

İlhan sorrowfully shook his head. "She knows," he said. "I tried so hard to not be with Ceren! I cursed myself . . ."

They extended their glasses towards each other. They clinked. İlhan started to explain, he had a great need to explain. He drew a scene, embellished with poetry and feelings of guilt. The scene came to life in Cemil's mind:

İlhan and Ceren were sitting across from each other in a pastry shop in Ümitköy. It was almost evening, the sun quickly descending towards the horizon, casting İlhan's shadow on the table, which was gradually approaching Ceren. My shadow is stretching out, keep stretching, İlhan thought to himself, keep stretching until it reaches the things that the İlhan of flesh and blood couldn't get to. He looked at Ceren's hands sitting on the table, then at her neck and her lips. When his shadow reached Ceren's eyes, the sun had set. Other things were being desired at different longitudes, because the world was spinning.

"A photographer if it was up to me!" said Ceren. "You know there are those creative photographers who go wandering around in the mountains, taking pictures of their feet. One of them."

İlhan laughed, but most of the time laughing was a kind of bribe. He knew that. He knew just how many gimmicks people sign up for in order to impress one another, in order to be loved, all the somersaults they'll do. We're never so lazy that we won't agree to set up and take down a giant circus every day. There are tightrope walkers, fire swallowers, clowns, dancing horses and of course lions in the ring. İlhan knew all of that. My shadow isn't just the banner of reined-in desire, fallen to the ground, thought İlhan. At the same time, it's evidence of the passage of time. I somehow couldn't believe that. It's actually the sign of the passage of time for all things, but I somehow couldn't believe that. And now I have to act ethically.

I can't think about Handan and Can even if I try. I can't think about how I'll look them in the face even if I try. Because time is passing us by, and morals have never saved anybody. They're just a rock tied to your foot. You go straight to the bottom. Straight down.

Only with literature would İlhan succeed in switching places with his shadow, with the type of clear-eyed literature that only Cortázar had managed to write.

Ceren gave a tense smile and looked at İlhan, who was caressing her hands on the table. But she didn't pull them away. That evening they had sex.

İlhan hoped that he could find the answers to some of his questions he had about himself there in between Ceren's legs. He thought, based on Freud, that men would find themselves in the place where they first lost themselves.

Was joy just the loss of memory, İlhan asked. If so, what could possibly be forgotten? Could he force himself to forget that man who got lost falling into garbage at the Mamak dump while collecting things to make money, whose family had spent all day looking for him, who had lit a fire and waited for him that night? The woman and young girl working at the side of the Muğla-Deniz highway selling mushrooms on a rainy night when only a few cars passed by—could they be forgotten? Could God, one of man's worst inventions, be forgotten? Could the ordinary be forgotten? By ordinary he meant life. Could the ordinary be forgotten?

Does wanting to use a young woman as a means to stop the passage of time, to take back from that body all of those things lost to time, to want it over and over again, does that make me a vampire?

"My teeth Ceren . . . are my teeth too much?" İlhan asks.

"Oh honey, you're so sweet," Ceren says, "if you want to bite me, bite me!"

32

The pesticide truck was driving around the apartment complex, a white cloud behind it. "Keep your children away from the pesticide truck!" the announcement was heard. Cemil closed the door to the balcony so that bugs wouldn't get in the apartment while escaping the pesticide. So that nothing from outside would enter the apartment. So that Cemil could live in the one-bedroom, one-living-room apartment amongst the books and music CDs while waiting for Nazlı to come back from work. So that he could read *Franny and Zooey* for the hundredth time. Not enough. For the one hundred and fiftieth time. To memorize *The Waves* line by line. To turn up the stereo and to listen to *Rumours*.

The sun was striking the kitchen counter. Cemil washed the dishes. He was moving the mop around in the bucket when he realized: there was sadness. A sadness you could account for, that you could balance out, written down in a big notebook, from an unknown source. People are alchemists: splinters, scratches, tiny little things could be morphed into sadness. The universe was full of matter, anti-matter, and sadness.

After Cemil washed the dishes, he called the apartment management. He waited patiently for the end of the recorded message. He asked the woman on duty who answered the phone with "Management!": "When will the energy meters in the Aktürk block be installed?" The woman on duty said the teams were in the Kutlutaş blocks, then they would go to Betontaş and AGE, and that they would make it to Aktürk at the end of the summer. "There'll be an announcement!" she said.

Even if it wasn't going to be for a few months, the thought of strangers coming into the apartment made Cemil feel restless. They were even going to come into the bedroom. Coming in and looking at the radiator in the bedroom. They would have to pull the closet a little to the side to take off the valves, but it was no big deal if the furniture was moved! Was it actually a big deal? Cemil was restless.

In the afternoon he called Metin. He got straight to it. "I don't want to meet that girl! I didn't say so yesterday, because I didn't want to upset İlhan, but I can't do it, man! How are we supposed to look at Handan or Can in the face if we did? I mean our man is in love, in the clouds. But us . . ."

"We're crawling on the ground!"

Metin was taken aback for a second. "Do you think we should meet her?"

"I can understand İlhan's excitement. But I also understand the need to protect his wife, his kid, and the value of the past they share. When a person can understand both those things at the same time, they don't know what to do."

"We gotta talk to him!" Metin said, "This is a thorn in all of our sides."

"I feel the same way. You know it's not like he's been complaining about a miserable home life or anything like that."

"Right, just complaining about the passing of time itself. Because time is more annoying than a wife or child. You know, tick tock tick tock tick tock!"

"Not to mention alarm clocks. You should come tonight if you want."

"Did you tell Nazlı?"

"I did." Cemil said.

"What did she say?"

"What *could* she say . . . nothing!"

33

Actually Nazlı had said something, but she had said it four years ago
on a summer night, that terrible summer when the water in the res-
ervoirs had begun to run out. The water hadn't been running for days,
and when it finally came back on, people flocked to buy barrels they
could fill. Terrible smells came up through the storm drains. The mayor
kept making announcements on the television. In his eyes you could
see the joy he felt in having something he had imagined for years
finally become a reality: the people in the city had turned into ghosts
and were wandering around in plain sight, carrying empty white barrels
in their hands.

That summer, Nazlı and Cemil had laid out their mattress on the
balcony, whispering to each other and falling asleep. They spoke about
the past. When the water eventually came back on, the memories were
left behind.

When Nazlı told Cemil that when she was a child her family used
to wash their hands with *Pril* detergent in the sink after eating fish, he
was totally shocked. It was alleged that the formula for unhappiness
was the same as that for dishwashing detergent. "Yes, you're right,
unhappiness, dish detergent, and sometimes laundry detergent . . ."
Nazlı said. She turned to Cemil and looked like she wanted to say
something else. Then she went on: "to try to cover up, to pretend you're
not the kind of person who eats fish . . . it's like feeling something but
trying not to feel it . . . to try to be somebody else . . . it always makes
you sad."

"I had hoped by a miracle I would get help becoming somebody
else, not from detergents," Cemil said. "One day I would get out of bed
and I'd be somebody else. Tom Braks, Superman, someone who could
dance and sing well, someone with wider shoulders, someone who was

like Jack Lemmon and Walter Matthau at the same time, someone who could play soccer well, someone who could fly kites for hours carefree, happy-go-lucky, a fool of the air."

Nazlı put her hand on Cemil's arm as if she wanted to stop him from going on with his sad list. But then, she herself added the saddest addendum of all, saying "to be young and in love again . . .".

They were silent. They looked a while at the light of the street lamps, believing that everything in the past had been very nice. It takes an empty stare to entertain empty beliefs.

"You still want all of those things!" Nazlı said.

"I do, but it was different back then!" said Cemil. "I marked the calendar, I set my sights on it, circled one of the days. I thought to myself, in the morning on that day I'll have become somebody else. Once my dad saw that I had marked one of the days and asked me 'do you have a test?' 'Yes, a test in physics!' I lied."

"In a way, you were telling the truth!" Nazlı said. "Everyone is waiting for a miracle, but they eventually have to confront the laws of physics."

At the end of summer, they brought in the mattress from the balcony.

34

The good thing about growing old together is knowing that you won't die because of something one of you did or didn't say to the other! When you're young, speaking and staying silent are both forms of betrayal. When they're young, people think they can easily take a life, and that it can easily be taken.

When Nazlı said that she wanted to be in love again, Cemil had been happy to see his wife express her human nature in such a natural and frank way. He aspired to be like her. He also liked the ways she was trying to show that she was in love, or trying not to be: pre-wash, cotton, ninety degrees. He didn't feel like he'd been betrayed. He didn't feel jealousy or anger. He wasn't surprised. Cemil wasn't naive or emotional. He felt sorry for her, of course. Sorry. But Cemil was a reader of literature. Readers of literature examine and operate on the people in each book they read. The knowledge that they acquire is larger than what you could gain merely through your own lived experience, and they understand everything about humans. They truly understand. Cemil had understood Nazlı and felt sorry for a version of Nazlı from the books he had read. Sorry.

Four years later, explaining to Nazlı that İlhan had a lover, Cemil said that even if it was coming from the mouth of a man who was married and had a kid, it was exciting to listen to his love story. What he didn't say was that it had re-awoken a desire in him to be in love again, and that for a while he had felt it as a deeply pressing need. He also didn't mention how seductive it was to think of the things he would find in the body of a young woman without having to look too hard.

Nazlı was also a reader of literature. Secretly she was hurt and offended. The cheerful crowd had slowly dispersed ever since the moment she learned about Cemil speaking with the editor, and Nazlı had been left completely alone in the world. In times like this, Nazlı always thought to herself: I only have my mom, only my mother loves me. She missed her smell. She wanted to cling to her and fall asleep.

The moment that Cemil first saw Berkan's girlfriend Şeyda, he thought to himself: now the story is going to speed up. Stories always speed up when a beautiful girl comes onto the scene.

Was the girl actually beautiful, or did she just seem that way to Cemil? Putting her beauty aside, Cemil didn't have the slightest idea whether or not the girl existed outside of his own perceptions. Or at least he wouldn't know for a little while longer. (As he was getting older, dry mouth was starting to rear its ugly head. It was compounded by the high voltage current of necessity, that was also a law of physics.) He could only hear a chirping, and sense that one of life's many stories had been brought and placed before him. Childhood can be spent happily or unhappily. That moment that you first feel different from other people, you get a glint in your eyes. You could still see that glint in this girl's big hazel eyes. Cemil imagined how those big eyes grew narrow whenever she was having sex. He thought how it was impossible for a girl like her to avoid seeing tigers in her dreams. The tiger entering her dreams was wild and erotic, ready to burst out into the open in one leap. The tiger in Berkan's dream, on the other hand, was probably just an image he'd seen on a patterned blanket.

Cemil invited his guests in.

Şeyda sat in the chair directly across from the bookcase and crossed her legs. Cemil thought to himself, alright, now the story will achieve a sort of contemporary realism. At that moment, without caring about her goofy boyfriend, she was telling her whole life story in such a way that Cemil could grab hold of one point and use it to draw himself in: Her mother was interested in literature. When she was young she got her book signed by a famous poet. Cemil asked which poet it was. Şeyda didn't remember. "We were living in Izmir at the time," she said.

Şeyda's father was an editor for a publisher that printed children's books. "Me, on the other hand, I sleepwalk." Şeyda explained, smiling, "I'm really interested in the East." She pointed at his bookcase as she said this. Cemil thought she meant that the books also seemed exotic.

As the girl spoke, Cemil looked her in the eyes and feigned ignorance. Cemil was avoiding making it seem like he was sitting there with bated breath, imagining the wet space between her legs, their groins rubbing against each other, and other types of general sexual commotion. Cemil knew that feigning ignorance was a kind of game. He felt as though he would feel the blood rush to his manhood at any moment. It made him uncomfortable to be sitting face to face with a girl. He turned to Berkan:

"Berkan you got anything new, are you writing?"

Berkan said he was working on a short film script. He was going to shoot it himself, and he wanted Şeyda to play the lead role. The girl laughed. Cemil saw it as a great sign of his maturity that Berkan wanted to shoot a short film rather than a full-length one. He offered them some AOÇ ice cream. They sat together for a few hours. Then all of a sudden, Şeyda said, "I'm bored!"

36

Cemil did his military service at the Ministry of National Defense.
Being a reserve officer was a lot like being a civil servant. He secretly
had a crush on his officemate Gülay. He couldn't take his eyes off her.
This small, middle-aged woman was definitely attractive, but Cemil's
attraction to her wasn't solely based on physical sexuality. Gülay was
bored all day, spreading out playing cards on her desk and reading her
fortune. Seeing her like that distracted Cemil. As Gülay turned over
the cards one by one, the lamp would slowly fade out, the sentence
would be read with acceptance, and there would be a sweet moaning
sound along with the five of spades, the nine of diamonds, the shirt
button, the bra clasp, her legs visible from inside her stockings. It was
the teeming sexuality of a woman who was so obviously bored. Bored
women always seemed to Cemil like they were just about to take their
clothes off. Cemil was young, there were no women in his life, so he got
excitement out of this interpretation. A few years later he would realize
that what had impressed him about this image wasn't merely that it
was sexy. A woman who read her fortune to save herself from boredom
was someone who jealously guarded her own time. Only someone who
possesses something can become bored with it. When Cemil realized
this, he also understood that he himself didn't have a single trace of
this relaxed attitude. He decided to convert to a new religion: He wore
bold, fashionable clothing that made him look dapper and bought a
deck of tarot cards. When he went home every evening, he'd read
his fortune for a long time at the dining table in the living room. He
drank tea, stroked the cards with his fingers, and spread them out on
the table without any sense of urgency. It was the second year of his
marriage to Nazlı. She was already used to him suddenly getting up
and going to the cemetery in Karşıkaya with his pet water bottle in

hand, and all of his other eccentricities. She watched her husband read his fortune without interrupting. People trying to remake themselves look ridiculous from the outside. Nazlı loved Cemil enough not to laugh at him.

This new ritual, of course, had no effect on his ability to control time, or on learning how to stop running around all over the place. All that happened was that Cemil got much faster at reading his own fortune!

37

"Ms. Editor, Seymour Glass in the story, "A Perfect Day for Bananafish"
leaves his room at the hotel to commit suicide but doesn't get away
without being scolded for furtively looking at the legs of a woman on
the elevator. At the same time, he does that thing that all good literary
characters do. He eloquently divides the world's people into two
groups: those who are like Seymour and those who aren't.

This is why we love protagonists: they help explain our "treacherous
and muddled" world through rough classifications, and in doing so
they show us distinctions we wouldn't have noticed. They point out
the things that have been divided by thinly drawn lines. It's good
for things to be well defined. Those who are like Raif Efendi in *The
Madonna in the Fur Coat* and those who are not. Those who are like
Oya in *Dawn* and those who are not. Those who are like Stephen
Dedalus and those who are not.

I did what I could so that the protagonist in my novel could be
used to divide the world's population in two. Believe me, I worked
really hard to do that. I used everything I've saved up in me, and
everything I haven't. That's because when you write a novel you
also use those things that don't belong to you as if they were yours.
You actually end up relying on them more. You act like you know
the things you don't know. The history of China, quantum physics,
Bakhtin's theory of literature, and Heidegger, of course. You act like
you know his work back to front. You come off as more just and
understanding than you are in real life. You are smart and brave.
Endlessly respectful.

Miss Editor, if I am able to exhibit these virtues while writing a novel,
and if it gets published, maybe I can hold onto them in my real life!
That's the most I can hope for.

If my novel gets published, I can stand up, unintimidated, against the magpies that chase me. I can finally confront Nedim, the man on duty I greet every morning when I go for the papers. And the neighborhood women whose voices echo in the empty space between the apartments, and who stare at me between the cracks in the door and through peep holes. And Nazlı's family. And I'll be able to do it all in proper attire. The attire of a writer. Not bad. At the very least it's better than walking around in my fencing outfit. Everyone in the apartment complex looks at me stand-offishly, like at any moment I'm going to pounce on them and activate a button on their chests that will shine an unflattering light onto their inner worlds.

If my novel gets published, perhaps the lack of talent I show on the soccer field can be vindicated in court. My inability to chest bump the soccer ball, the fact that I never use my right foot, my awfulness at playing midfield—all will be forgiven. It will no longer pose a problem of conscience that I quit my job and stayed at home without reading books, without writing a single sentence, just spending hours a day daydreaming. Maybe I'll be able to listen to "Sensitive Kind" by John Mayall or "Sinnerman" by 16 Horsepower over and over again without tearing up. Maybe I'll be able to make strawberry jam without being overtaken by morbid feelings. Maybe even peach jam.

What's more, if my novel gets published, I'll be a more attractive man.

I expect so much from a book, don't I Miss Editor? Just as much as I expect from women."

Şeyda was a beautiful girl, but the story wasn't speeding up! In later encounters, Cemil slowly began to realize that the girl actually did exist outside of his own perceptions, and that she was beautiful. She had a great body, the kind that brings to mind a plump fruit. A well-shaped face, which brought to mind an oval mirror with a flowery porcelain frame. And this comparison to a mirror was on purpose: the only thing that Şeyda seemed capable of in a human relationship was reflecting back the blurry image of whoever stood across from her. That was it. Every time Cemil looked at the girl, he saw a beauty that dazzled him, but there was no other positive attribute to be seen.

Şeyda came along with Berkan a few times. Then she even came by herself, using the excuse of the book *The Soda Tree*. It was obvious that it was an excuse. "last time we came, we were going to give it back, but we forgot, I left it in my bag," she explained while displaying it histrionically. Maybe she didn't know how to act either. "Berkan has been acting really jealous recently," she said abruptly, then she put her hand on her cheek and said she didn't feel well, that her blood pressure might be low. Cemil measured the girl's blood pressure, but he really didn't like the way she stretched out her arm as if she was entrusting a lamb to a wolf. He, the old wolf, squinted and withdrew into the misty depths of his own impossible forest. Then he got really quiet, made a sullen expression, and said almost nothing. But it was impossible to speak to Şeyda anyhow. She used a limited range of vocabulary, swimming the crawl through a narrow library, speaking about herself and the things she "totally" loved and "totally" hated, boasting about her own eccentric personality. When Cemil or Berkan would begin to speak, she'd glance around with a vacant expression. Only one time, as Cemil explained how he quickly ate bread and cheese to make sure that the smell of the egg he ate before breakfast didn't contaminate his tea. Şeyda had jumped in to say "tomatoes! Tomatoes also get rid of the smell of egg." The girl clearly thought that everyone was enamored of her. Most of the world is divided up between those people who think everyone is enamored of them, and those who think that nobody loves them. The rest are those who read Vüs'at O. Bener.[2]

That day, as Cemil saw Şeyda off, he knew that he wouldn't be seeing much of the young couple anymore. Or at least Şeyda wouldn't want to see him. The story resumed its former, sluggish flow.

---

[2] Turkish novelist, short story writer, and poet (1922-2005)

BARIŞ BIÇAKÇI

When Cemil stopped to think about it, he realized that Nazlı was going to leave him. He was even excited, picturing the scene in his mind: Cemil on the ground, Nazlı bent forward and holding out her hand as she was ready to leave, her curly hair falling on her cheeks, her neck resembling a bird's nest, a sense of compassion in her eyes, like a longing for distant mountains. But in this scenario, waiting behind Nazlı was a whole line of other women, ready to reach their hands out to Cemil. A line of identically calm women stretching out to the horizon; it was like they had always been there, since Cemil had been born. Standing there ready to fill an echoless void.

As much as Cemil tried, he couldn't erase the image of these women that had come to life in his mind. He didn't like that he was becoming one of those men interested in harems, and he performed philosophical somersaults to avoid taking responsibility for where his imagination was leading. Life was expansive and there was more of it than there needed to be. He felt like enormous numbers were being whispered into his ear. Nine hundred and forty-four women, for example, sixty-three thousand books, one hundred thousand seas, one million beers . . . sitting on the balcony happily drinking tea, he could still hear someone whispering into his ear that there were one billion other tea bags in cups just like this one waiting for him somewhere else. Sitting beside them were lentil patties and apple cookies, it said. I am imagining things, Cemil thought, just so that I don't go insane thinking about all of life's meaningless, overwhelming richness and promises. This blurry expanse, this echoless void. I am trying to fill my imagination with visual echoes. How else do I cope with the voice trying to belittle the things I possess, the moments I've lived, insisting that there are so many other things that could be experienced instead? Either I become someone who can be consoled by their own imagination, or I end up fighting against everything I see. It's so hard to be human!

Cemil thought about what made him find all of these women so appealing. He realized that he was picturing them at precise moments. Moments when they gave him looks, when they tried to flirt with him, those dizzying moments when they touched or were having sex. The appeal of these imaginary women was actually based on the idea that all of these single pleasurable moments could simply be gathered up together. That's what people want to believe: let me collect pleasurable things just as I would gather up delicious apples and delicious pears please! Cemil knew that he had really achieved a sense of continuity by collecting these moments from his life in his mind, but in fact what is actually consistent in life is that memories are both steadily being added together and then subtracted.

Cemil thought about this, he understood it, he knew it. But the women were still there. They loved life, they were happy with their situation, and when they set their eyes on Cemil, they were ready and waiting for a small sign from him to push Nazlı aside.

One early Sunday evening, Nazlı told Cemil: "Look at what you're doing to me!" It was the beginning of July. It hadn't gotten dark out yet, and the evening sun was filling the living room.

Cemil had the newspaper spread out on the living room table, sorting out the greens he had bought at the store. Parsley, arugula, dill. He was of course sorting them like a man from the city would. Without paying enough attention. Even being kind of harsh.

When Nazlı had finished her work in the kitchen and came into the living room, she saw the fresh, bright green pieces of parsley and arugula that he had sorted out, and she lost it. How could Cemil slaughter her beloved greens! Didn't he know how valuable parsley, arugula, and all other kinds of greens were to Nazlı?

"Look at what you're doing to me!"

Accepting the blame, Cemil watched closely as Nazlı went back over the greens and called out each time she sorted one. His wife's hands were kind and compassionate.

One day in the first year of their marriage, in the spring when the sun had come out after a hard rain, Nazlı had wandered around the slopes of the hill around the heating center, picking greens by scraping at their roots with a wooden-handled knife, just like her mother had taught her. She found twenty-two types of plants. As she sorted out the plants she had picked, she told Cemil their names one by one. "This is evelik, this is tekesakalı, this is güvercin topu . . ." Then she roasted an onion and added cracked wheat and cooked the greens. Cemil ate the dish that Nazlı said was called Yazı pancarı where she was from, and he realized that for her, greens were the feeling of security, the security of having her mother at her side to bring her a glass of water.

The greens were something that unashamedly linked Nazlı to her childhood and family, and the food's astringent taste came straight from the past.

Nazlı had spent her childhood in a coastal city. From their balconies, between geraniums planted in olive oil canisters, they could see the sea, large freight ships, small fishing boats, and skiffs that resembled house slippers. The rooms had a deep blue light. Nazlı went on walks in the evening, drank lightly sugared tea, and fell asleep in her father's lap. Time passing through the eye of a needle, embroidery sewn onto the broad white cloth of childhood.

Nazlı also explained how that embroidery had come apart.

They barely made ends meet. Her father wanted their youngest child Nazlı to go to school. He saw to it too, and took an interest in her studies. After elementary school, Nazlı took her exams and got into the middle school where all the city's rich kids went. But she had to keep some things hidden while she was there: her breasts, which kept growing with each passing day, her family, their house, even the neighborhood where they lived. The village they went to in the summer . . .

Nazlı explained all of this in one breath. Cemil said that humankind's greatest achievement would be to create a system where children wouldn't have to live worrying about ridiculous things like that. "Socialism!" he shouted out in excitement; he gave Nazlı a nice big kiss.

That Sunday evening, he also got up and kissed Nazlı's slender wrists as she sorted out the greens, then embraced her from behind. He sunk his nose into the nape of her neck, and cupped her breasts. Nazlı started to laugh. Cemil held onto her and took her to bed. A little later, things they remembered were mixed together with things they forgot, that essential blend which produces human beings.

41

Cemil felt a deep sense of guilt for wanting to fall in love. He started to picture Nazlı as a young girl in his dreams. These were powerful, moving dreams which would suddenly came back to him throughout the day. They weren't the type of ridiculous flashes where something important or some truth suddenly came to light, but Cemil still always woke up from them flustered, captivated by some aspect of them. Then he would embrace Nazlı.

The thing that all of these dreams had in common was the four or five-year-old version of Nazlı running towards him.

One of these times Cemil was at the sea. He was standing motionless in the water, looking at the shoreline. At that moment, he saw Nazlı between the lounge chairs, dressed in red overalls. Nazlı also saw Cemil, running towards him on a long wooden pier. Coming to the end of the pier, there was nothing but open air and water, but she kept running without noticing. She took a step into the air, falling into the sea like a toy doll. In a panic, Cemil pulled her out of the water and grabbed onto her. She looked lovingly, excitedly at Cemil with her wet hair matted against her head, her moonlike face, bright-eyed Nazlı, without noticing that she had fallen in or that she had swallowed water. Then she said "You know what Cemil? On the way over here I threw up four times in the car!"

In another dream, Nazlı and Cemil were going to the market in the apartment complex. Right as Nazlı was about to walk into the store she asked to play with the kids on the playground. She said to Cemil "you go, I'm going to play here!" and started playing with her friends. Cemil went into the store and started wandering the aisles when he saw Nazlı come in through the door and run to his side. Nazlı pressed Cemil's hand, her small chest quickly rising and falling. She regretted leaving Cemil to go play. She looked at him, asking for forgiveness, quickly fitting herself into a space on the shelf where the honey jars were lined up.

In another one, Nazlı was running from the bedroom into the living room and, seeing Cemil writing something at the table, asked "What are you doing!" between breaths.

Cemil answered, "I'm talking to my dad."

Nazlı pointed at the photograph on the wall and said, in surprise, "But he's dead!" Then, sensing she knew nothing about this world, she asked "can we talk to the dead?" Stepping on her tippy toes, she looked at the pen in Cemil's hand and the papers in front of him and saw them as tools for speaking to the dead. With the confidence of someone who had just learned a secret, she said "I'm going to speak to them too!" She put close to her mouth the pieces of paper she had picked up from the table, and shouted like she was speaking to a deaf person: "My best friend Cemil and Nazlı, Cemil and Nazlı!"

42

Summer came and there were no secrets left.

The people living in the apartment complex spent most of their time on their balconies. They ate breakfast and dinner on the balcony. Tea spoons, porcelain plates, the cracking sound of sunflower seeds, table games and the sound of dice, conversations echoing against the surfaces of the buildings and reverberating everywhere. Husbands and wives arguing, children always crying in the same position, a man explaining to the person across from him how difficult his life was, a young girl speaking on the telephone who began by yelling and then starting to cry . . . when people go quiet, the summer sky begins to shed its secrets, like spears in the daytime and stars in the night.

Cemil also ate his breakfast on the balcony. He didn't come inside until the sun had moved to the West and was shining onto the balcony. He read books, wrote various things on the fold-out table. A diary. Sometimes sentences too. If only I had put this in the novel, my novel which I still haven't heard anything about, he thought regretfully. But more often than not, he listened to Mrs. Nermin in number six reading the newspaper to her mother. Mrs. Nermin read the newspaper out loud slowly so that her mother would understand. Cemil was actually annoyed listening to the woman's voice, which made everything comprehensible. It added insult to injury that everything could be understood. But he couldn't stop listening. The stupidest political debates, the strangest intrigues, the most inhumane things. First the woman would read the headlines on the first page. "Surprise Visitor at the Palace" "Military Measure Not a Solution" "Ministry Statement: Those Opposed to Hydro Project Shouldn't Use Electricity!" Then she moved on to the opinion columns. "Try looking at the picture this way. We will see a Turkey that has matured to the point of being able to resolve its problems through democratic means." She turned a few pages. First she read the menu of the Prime Minister's Iftar dinner. "An Iftar dish, lentil soup, cheese pastry, stew, rice, compote and caramelized milk pudding with ice cream." Then she listed out one by one what the leader of the opposition party had eaten at their Iftar dinner. Everything was completely comprehensible. Cemil could understand it. Mrs. Nermin turned a few more pages. "Research on Infinity," she said, and took a deep breath. "In a recent study conducted by Boston University, people explained what they understood by the word infinity. In the experiment, groups of people from different age and professional groups were asked what images came to mind when they heard the word infinity. The participants, who were unable to hear one another's responses, all described the emptiness of space. They spoke about a wide expanse of darkness punctured by starlight, complete silence, and the limitless universe. The most shocking thing about their descriptions was that each one of the participants imagined themselves moving at a high speed through the emptiness of space and, while moving at such a speed, they described the things they thought they could see. Meteors coming straight for them, planets appearing and disappearing all at once. They passed through fields of vision containing billions of stars in mere seconds. The researchers drew a parallel between the physical structure of the universe and the fact that people could only imagine infinity while being in a state of movement. They say that we have internalized the fact that everything in the universe is in a state of motion, and therefore it is natural for our visions of infinity to include motion."

Nonsense! Cemil leaned over the balcony and called out. "Mrs. Nermin, don't confuse your mother's brain with ridiculous thoughts. All of those spaceships, moving through emptiness! Such nonsense!"

Just as Cemil was about to share his ideas about his own relationship with eternity, he could see a few mathematicians working on the road that passed in front of the heating center. Anything is possible in the summertime. It was clear that the mathematicians were excited. Mathematicians are always excited; everything excites them. The variables x and y, for example, square roots, and then zero, even zero can excite them. Mathematicians draw straight, simple lines. They write that one end of the line is negative infinity and the other end is positive infinity. It's a number line. Mathematically infinite. Everything is possible, do you understand? Then they draw a circle tangential to this number line. Then, by matching the top point of the circle with a random point on the number line, they show how each point on the right corresponds to a single point on the circle, and similarly, any point on the circle corresponds to a single point on the number line.

Mathematicians are patient, they love matching one to one. By doing this, they were matching up an infinite number line with something that was enclosed, with a circle. When Cemil saw this, he was quite pleased. He loved things that were finite, enclosed, and circular. He understood that infinity and life were both circular, that without moving you could reach the infinite, and that this was a great secret. Yes, when summer came there were no more secrets left.

The cushions that had been placed in between the window sills so that the open windows wouldn't slam shut were slouching: the buildings were sticking out their tongues.

Cemil started taking his walks around the first floor at night. The weather was really hot. Sometimes Nazlı came with him.

One night, they went out around eleven o'clock. They walked fast. With their windows lit up, the apartments looked like an illuminated ferry. "The apartment complex is slowly pulling into the dock." Cemil said. The lights of the street lamps and the headlights of the cars occasionally passing by made some things visible out in the night, while other parts were pushed into darkness and became invisible. A hot breeze wound around Nazlı and Cemil's arms, the trees swayed, the leaves began to rustle. The sky was hung up by its four corners, shaken out, spread wide open. Somewhere far away, fireworks went off then disappeared. They passed by trees whose flowers smelled like bathroom soap during the first days of spring. They thought about the other smells that lingered in the apartment complex from the first days of spring until the end of summer: the bathroom soap tree, acacia, wisteria, honeysuckle, linden, oleaster, rose and then honeysuckle once again because fall is just another version of spring. Nazlı said that the apricots from Iğdır weren't sweet. Cemil was more understanding. "The good ones are good!" he said. They heard the long, distant, lovely whistle from a train passing behind the Betontaş Block, and saw a small, dark blue prison bus passing in front of them. It was traveling slowly, with the dexterity of an armored car, iron bars covering its small windows up to the roof.

Nazlı and Cemil didn't think they were lucky to not be imprisoned themselves, their noses pressed up against the iron windows inside the minibus on that summer night, that they were free instead to walk with their hands and arms swinging, able to talk about nice smells and apricot trees.

As a matter of fact, they initially felt nothing. They just stood there. Then they began feeling the pain they had known for years. The photographs in newspapers, and the sights and sounds from television all took the form of a knife, its steel glow spreading out and stabbing their left shoulders. The prison bus stopped. The back door opened. Out came women with their hair and faces burned, their mouths agape at the terrible shock they had experienced, their eyes pitch black. Smothered in ointment, wrapped up in cloth, half-naked, they began running towards the apartment complex. They were screaming. To let everyone know: THE STATE IS A KILLER! THE STATE IS A BUTCHER! THE STATE IS FOR THE RICH!

That night, they saw through all the magic tricks and illusions our daily lives use to distract us. The stark contrast between life and death, between people and the state, became visible.

Nazlı and Cemil looked on at this contrast. But they couldn't look for long.

They squinted their eyes. They looked away.

"Ms. Editor, the fact that we're still alive despite so much pain is either due to the fact that we're a bunch of hustlers, or because we still have hope. Me, personally, I feel like a hustler.

Ms. Editor, have you heard of Max Beckmann? He was a German painter who lived between 1884-1950, who witnessed the terror of the twentieth century firsthand, and who was unable to remain indifferent to it. He said, "to live with intense feelings is the same as creating new artistic forms. It is the foundation of form." Anger, pain, terror, loneliness, fear, constriction, anxiousness . . . how can a painting which uses the repulsive color equivalents of these feelings, one that tries to convey these distorted shapes, how can it still be beautiful? Beckmann was successful because he knew that by focusing on form he could be saved from the tyranny of the things he had witnessed.

To get into a discussion about form today, you have to be able to use a lot of jargon and come off as deep. It's obvious that modern society does not welcome or want people to have intense feelings. That's why we have doctors and medication. And we have friends to let us know that life will go on no matter what.

It is expected that we bear witness and stay silent, without under-taking any new search for forms of our pain or for that of others. And it's not because the world today is not a more wholesome place than Beckmann's was. Everything is trying to proliferate beyond all limits: people, weapons, and money.

When we look at life today, we see the reign of garbage and murder, the terrible and embarrassing poetry about minarets and bayonets, we see the imposing monuments to dirty wars. Literature is slowly becoming a luxury item. Writing under these circumstances means

BARIŞ BIÇAKÇI

that you only get one good chance to strike a deathblow. Anything beyond that and you're just trying to hustle people.

As I was writing the novel that I submitted to your publishing house, I kept searching and searching for that single deathblow. But now I'm thinking that my writing . . .

When I was five, I got in a taxi with my mother and father to go to my circumcision ceremony. I was holding on to my mother's hand. I was scared. My father turned to me from the front seat and told me that it wouldn't hurt a bit. "It'll just feel like a mosquito bite!"

No, I couldn't find the right way to strike! I am not a writer, Ms. Editor, I am a mosquito bite author. If you publish my book please write a warning on the back cover for readers: it won't hurt a bit!

Sincerely . . ."

Forugh Farrokhzad's memoir *In an Eternal Sunset* was published in 1989 by Ada Publishers. They published 1,600 copies, numbered each one of them, and put a black and white photo of Forugh on the cover. Even though the photo was grainy, a person would still be struck by the poet's big beautiful eyes, her plump lips, and her smile as she leaned her head slightly towards her right shoulder.

As he looked at the photograph of Forugh, Cemil thought that poets had to adopt their own methods, different from those of other people, if they wanted to survive. That smile was her single and definitive act of self-defense. He opened the book and read a poem while standing there. The poem was great. It made him want to head straight home. For Cemil, this was the most dependable measure of beauty: the beautiful was that which made you want to return home. Taking the book and heading to the checkout, the desire to return home grew even stronger: he saw Nazlı. They were smiling, holding hands.

"Cemil, this is Hale!" Nazlı said, "Hale is my roommate." Cemil was surprised that Nazlı still remembered his name months later, even though they had only spoken one time in the hospital room, and it had been rushed and awkward. It made him happy. Hale suggested they go to the Yüksel coffeeshop.

"Sounds good, we'll have tea, let's go!" Nazlı said.

While sitting at the coffee shop, Hale said that she already knew Cemil.

"Well, don't know you . . . I've seen you in front of the SSC!"

A few years before, when Cemil was in his last year of university, he and his friends had gone to a big demonstration in Kızılay where the police had intervened and arrested dozens of students. İlhan was among those who got arrested. After being interrogated in the

　　BARIŞ BIÇAKÇI

police department, the students were moved to the State Security Court. Cemil and Metin and a group of students camped out in the street around the SSC, waiting for those who had been arrested to be released from the court.

Hale turned and asked Nazlı: "you remember, don't you?"

Nazlı said, "I remember, of course! But I didn't meet Cemil there. We met later, in the hospital . . ." She was looking into Cemil's eyes.

Cemil was surprised, "You were in front of the court too? What were you doing there?"

"What do you mean what was I doing there? We were waiting for our friends too!"

They spoke about what they could still remember from those days. Cemil couldn't forget the music blaring from a tape cassette brought by one of the kids from the group waiting in front of the court. "Pink Floyd, Dire Straits, they were playing stuff like that all day long. I think they even played Paul Simon's *Graceland*. They walked around collecting money for batteries." They all laughed. Hale laughed too much. "That kid became my boyfriend later on!" she said.

"But it only lasted two months!" Nazlı added. "Cemil, you read a poem there . . ."

"'They're Coming from the Wilderness'" Cemil said, "a poem by Turgut Uyar . . . Why didn't you say that you knew me at the hospital?"

Nazlı opened her hands up and stuck out her lower lip. A shiver passed through Cemil.

"Yes, 'They're Coming from the Wilderness' . . . you read it so well!" Hale said.

They spoke about their friends who had been arrested. Then they asked each other what they did. Nazlı had finished school, she had taken another specialization exam, she was waiting for the results. She wanted to be an internist. Hale still had a year before she finished school, she didn't know yet whether or not she wanted to go into medicine. "But if I do, I won't get all stuck up," she said. Cemil also spoke about himself. He explained how he had done his military service working as a reserve officer in a ministry. "Yeah look, his hair is gone!" Nazlı said. Hale was sad to hear that Cemil had lost his father; she asked about his mother. When Hale heard that she had died when he was six, right then and there she turned into Cemil's mother, the one who hadn't been alive for eighteen years. Women can simultaneously try to be both a mother and a small girl.

Nazlı preferred to be a young girl.

"Are you on your own now?" Hale asked. "Like, you have no relatives?"

"Blood relatives, no," Cemil said. He told them about Metin and İlhan. The three of them wrote poetry and saw each other a lot. "We're a good trio!"

Nazlı pointed at the plastic bag from the bookstore and asked "what did you buy, a poetry book?" Cemil took the book out and handed it to Nazlı. "I came across a really good poem while I was standing there flipping through it."

He showed Nazlı the page with the poem "The Bird is Mortal" on it. Hale also leaned in from where she was sitting. As the two women read the poem together, Cemil looked on, admiring Nazlı's hand as it held onto the book.

BARIŞ BIÇAKÇI

When Nazlı read a book, she underlined parts, wrote sentences or words she liked on little pieces of paper, and took notes on the last page of the book. As she turned the pages, she felt like she was moving away from certain feelings, from an impression, and she would often go back and reread what she had read. The book became Nazlı's nest.

Cemil looked on jealously as her eyebrows appeared and then disappeared again like a bird lifting her head out of the nest.

For Cemil, reading wasn't something you did by yourself. It was something else, something more. It was a height he couldn't reach, a distance he couldn't get to. He couldn't get into the things he read; his mind wandered, he'd get back up as soon as he had sat down. When this happened, Cemil felt like the sentences were acting conceited about the secrets they concealed. He tried reading more slowly. He tried stopping, thinking. But despite all of this, soon after finishing a book he would have already forgotten a bunch of things about it. Which story was it with the man going to the bus station with his father and they're about to meet his sister, then when he opens up to his sister at the seaside, what was it they talked about? Was that university professor — he knew all too well which book he was in — forcing his student to sleep with him, or did the girl like him too?

When he picked a book he'd read back up, trying to remember, he'd turn the pages and feel more sure of its details, but also more sure he was a failure.

But there were some books, books that he had really gotten into, books that showered him with an amazing feeling of evenness. He felt a simple joy. A joy which made everything simple. This light. This page. This tea. Olive oil, onions and bread. Raisins and roasted chickpeas. A small wooden table. That bottle. Two chairs. A Faulkner.

One evening late at night after Cemil finished *As I Lay Dying* and sat in the darkness with the table lamp turned off, Faulker showed up, like all good writers do, with a candle in his hand. He looked into Cemil's eyes: he was trying to see whether or not Cemil also saw the complexity of the living world. The shadows cast on the walls of the apartment by the candle looked on impatiently alongside him.

Outside, the area containing hundreds of apartments in the complex was silent, dark. Like they were being silent and dark in order to hide the complexity of the living world, like they had been built right on top of all that complexity.

In the mid-two-thousands, when people in the residential block area of town would pass by Susuz Lake, they'd see a sign hanging at the entrance to Göksu Park; a little park that they had made out of the land surrounding the lake by encircling it with a fence. People would see the sign that read "This place used to be full of drunks, it's not clear exactly who did what, but now look how pretty it is!" Then they'd look at the lake and immediately be convinced that this was true. Big lies always seem to win people over.

The drunks used to drive their automobiles up to the top of the lone hill overlooking the entrance to the housing block, where you could see the ring road they built after pulling out all the trees that used to be at the edge of the lake, and they'd look out at the view of new buildings stretching out uninterrupted into the distance as far away as Sincan, and they'd of course watch the sunset, and drink rakı and think to themselves: what's happening? Later, they would ask themselves again: what happened?

In the beginning, buildings had just a single floor, everything was at ground-level. Then what happened? Then they began building second stories. All of the different-sized hills were flattened out. They put up tall buildings. On the first floor in front of the telephone booths, there would be a crowd of workers gathered to make phone calls to their families, in guttural voices, in another language.

It was empty around Susuz Lake, and in order to stand the emptiness you had to drink rakı. One winter day it rained like crazy, and the lake overflowed. The overflowing water covered a wide area and then poured into the street from next to a one-story post office. For the next few days people and workers from the block housing were picking up fish that were flopping around, with their bare hands and plastic bags. They bought lettuce at the store. Onions. Halvah. Dinner.

In the beginning there was the first floor, the second floor, and the frogs. So many frogs. Walking at night, there were frogs hopping around left and right. Then there were lots of frog deaths. They got caught underneath automobiles and learned what it was like to be one of those little paper origami frogs. The number of automobiles went way up, the parking lots filled up, and the frogs completely disappeared. A few hedgehogs would wander around at night. They wandered around on the roads, in the parks. They wandered around in silence, deep in thought. When they came across a human they'd say "ah!" and bounce up on their tiny little feet. They were very slow; they'd curl up into themselves and would also get caught underneath automobiles.

In the fall, the beet trucks would line up in front of the sugar factory. When the winter snow began to fall, the municipal buses couldn't get back up the inclines. On summer nights, sprinklers would spin around watering lawns. It was hard to walk without getting wet. People thought water was plentiful. The sound of cicadas sounded a lot like the sound of the sprinklers.

The people living in the block housing started to get annoyed about the workers because they didn't fit in with the surroundings. They were everywhere, in the minibuses, on the regular buses, in the store . . . they smelled bad, they spoke in their own languages, they scared children, their faces were unshaven. The three, four, and five-story buildings started being built over this fear. A nice big increase. Fear spurs growth.

Then what happened? Then the people from the housing block started hanging flags from their windows. They hung up CDs to scare away pigeons that were trying to make nests on their balconies. When the CDs moved in the wind, white and blue lights would flicker inside their homes, on the walls, the tables, on the tiles, and over their faces.

Then what happened? Then trans people started living on the newly built floors. At night they would go looking for clients in the streets. The people in the housing block attacked them with shawarma knives and baseball bats; they beat the shit out of them and chased them off. The police only stood by and watched. Once the frogs, hedgehogs, pigeons, stinking workers and trans people were all gone, they could start more quickly with the construction of fancier apartments, business parks, and malls.

Then what happened, the drunks thought. The sun was just about to set behind the buildings over in Sincan. Then, on the hill that had the first-floor heating station, they lit up a thousand little lights which made the shape of a Turkish flag. The flag was like a billboard; in the evening they'd turn on the lights, and the orangish-red and white lights looked like a star and crescent. Then some of the lights stopped working. At night, a dark band appeared in the middle of a flag. After that, all of the lights broke. Then the flag, both at night and in the daytime, looked like the ruins of a country that had invaded itself.

After finishing his military service, Cemil had married Nazlı and had started working for a large construction company in downtown Ankara. The company made irrigation dams, ponds, and irrigation channels. The treads and large tires of the construction equipment crushed eryngo, bluebottles, poppies, upturned the soil, knocked mountains and hills down with help from dynamite, uprooted trees, rolled stones out of the way. The two fox cubs paced around their dead mother, not knowing what to do.

Cemil's job, from the point of view of the ecosystem, consisted of drawing up job proposals and work plans for how best to kill the mother fox. In the first year of the job, he went to Eastern Anatolia to visit their construction sites and to obtain information related to field engineering. He liked traveling and relished that special joy reserved for engineers, but also enjoyed by all Homo Sapiens: the joy of fighting against nature and subduing it.

At the end of the first year, he felt he had gotten used to working in the company. He was a good engineer. He took the initiative in projects he was interested in, and easily came up with excuses to go to the building sites and stay there for a while. He really loved the feeling of being someone who had spent their whole life in Ankara but who was now on the road. That wild feeling of not belonging: there were clouds, mountains, and plains. I can keep going forward, I can head back. The letters and numbers written on the blue road signs, framed with white lines, were so satisfying and familiar to Cemil that they felt like pages of a book scattered to the four corners of the country. He read this book with excitement. The gas stations, the roadside restaurants, the tea houses, and even the foul-smelling bathrooms on his trips made it feel like he was inside a story. The view from a small, shoddily constructed window, without any glass, inside a stinking bathroom with a flimsy roof and an open door. Framed, illuminated beauty. Resplendent and spectacular. *Come on let's go.*

Everything at the worksite was covered in dust during the day. The sound of the machines rattled your brain. Then break time came, everything was stopped, turned off. The sky was approaching with its head down like a wild animal accustomed to eating out of a human's hand. The trees that had been hiding suddenly appeared, the curves in the footpaths were smoothed out, the mountains stood like they always did, and the sounds of crickets and frogs began: life goes on, life goes on.

Before dark, Cemil walked around the places where "there were few humans and lots of God" like Sadri Alışık says in that one film, swelling up his chest and taking deep breaths, both the past and the future in this breath. In the soft light of the evening, Cemil felt that the various pieces that made up this scene were all acquainted. The plants knew the rocks; the lizards knew the purple cloud; the mountains knew the humans and Cemil knew the folk song: *Even if the bird's wing was my pen, my pain could not be written.*

One evening while walking around and looking at the view he wondered: "Is nature missing anything?" He answered himself with "if it is, I know what could make it whole: literature!" Cemil loved rhyme, and art was for art's sake after all.

He loved the awareness that nature gave him. Coming in contact with all of these things made him more sensitive. He wanted to write poetry or a novel, to return back home, to hug Nazlı. He blended the three things together: Nazlı, home, and literature.

During the twelve years that Cemil worked as a construction engineer he had seen the courses of many rivers changed. He had seen their rushing water slowed. And, after being collected behind the massive concrete walls, he'd seen their death. The grandeur of concrete began to bother him, he could sense in it an arrogant threat.

Watching the slope of the land, he loved the irrigation canals and how they sometimes reflected the sky, sometimes the weeping willow trees. They always reminded him of Orhan Kemal's novels. Kind of sad, kind of gritty.

His worksite trips trailed off in his last days at the company. But whenever he would get five or six loquats or a few strawberries in his lunch, Cemil wanted to hit the road again, to be in nature. Looking at the seasonal, fully ripe fruit on his metal cafeteria tray made him feel like nature stood half-way between life and death, and that he too needed to be standing at the same point, there alongside the irrigation canals.

That day started slowly. But then everything happened all at once.
Cemil almost missed the match.

After breakfast in the morning, he listened to the radio for a bit. From the window, he watched the number 541 bus struggling its way up the slightly winding incline. In the morning hours, almost nobody came from the city into the apartment complex. The bus was practically empty; the small group of passengers, without showing a single sign of life, passed by in front of his window. The large window shook imperceptibly.

Around noon, while hanging up the laundry, he called İlhan. They spoke for a long time. İlhan was being crushed under the movie script's worth of lies he had been forced to tell Handan in order to be with Ceren. "Is it worth going through all of this deceit just to suck a young girl's blood?" he asked. "I don't know," Cemil said, "I really don't know. Somewhere I read that human blood has about the same chemical composition as seawater. Blood is our reminder that all life originated in the ocean. So of course a girl's blood has a similar effect!" There was a pause. "What do you mean?" İlhan asked. There was another pause, then İlhan said "I guess I understand." See you tonight they said and hung up.

Cemil hung up the remaining laundry. He looked at how it flapped in the breeze and thought about how much he loved İlhan's used of the word "weightless," how he used it all the time in the poetry he wrote when he was young, but how somehow it had never made his poems too light. Just three friends coming together having fun, telling funny jokes one after another. Cemil remembered one night while they were walking he had suddenly stopped and put his foot up on a low garden wall and stared at the full moon. Then, noticing that his shoe was in position for getting a shine, he had said in a pompous way "hey there, come shine my shoe, will ya?" He laughed to himself.

He made tea. He looked at the teaspoon section in the drawer and saw all of the ones Nazlı had thought were nice and had stolen from hotels when she went to medical seminars. Around ten teaspoons, none of which resembled one another. It really was great. He called Nazlı and told her he loved her so much, "because of the teaspoons!" Nazlı laughed.

Then the phone rang again. This time it was Cem, asking for help with an engineering term he had come across in a book he was translating. Cemil said "actually they use the term gravitational, you know? Gravitational water transport. But you could also use elevated. Elevation." While hanging up, Cem said, "one second! Mira wants to speak with you." Mira picked up the phone. "At school today they taught us why cakes rise, Cemil!" she said. Then, sounding like a teacher, he asked himself "why do cakes rise?" Cemil repeated the question a few times, like he was thinking about it, "Well it must be because of the moon's gravity, isn't it? Just like the ocean. It's the same for cakes, because of the tides, they puff up." On the other side of the line there was an exasperated groan. Then came a deafening scream: "Baking powder!"

Cemil turned on the television around two o'clock while he was eating lunch. They were showing old reruns during the daytime. He flipped to one of the episodes from the first season of the series *The Sultan's Quarters*, which had come out years ago, and he really got into it. He liked the episode so much that he suddenly wanted for the book version to come out. Life was a banquet Cemil was invited to, but Cemil was uneasy because he had come to the banquet empty-handed, he couldn't enjoy it. He thought about calling the publisher. He decided not to.

He washed the dishes. He exchanged glances with the pigeons who had made a nest on the adjoining apartment roof, closing one eye and looking askance at the birds. He laughed. The birds weren't paying attention.

A little later there was a knock on the door, Berkan told him that the downstairs apartment had been emptied. His grandmother was still in the hospital and in intensive care, she couldn't breathe, they had given her a tracheotomy. There was no chance she was going to get better, but she was still alive. Berkan said "I'll still come by once in a while, Mr. Cemil," sounding withdrawn and distant.

When Cemil prepared his bag for the game it was four o'clock. When he thought about Berkan's grandmother, he remembered the story "The End of Something", and wanted to read it again. He picked up *Summerhouse, Later* and laid down on the couch. Lying on his left ear to read the right page, his right ear to read the left, he reread the story five years later.

He left the apartment at ten past five. He waited for a long time for the bus that went to the Batıkent metro station. When the bus finally came, Cemil had become anxious. After inserting his card in the machine, he looked at the time written on it: it was twenty-five before six. I'll be in Batıkent at five before six, he thought. On the bus he asked a few people if they had the time. He got on the metro at six. At six-fifteen he arrived at Kızılay station, running over to the Ankaray side, then up the stairs. The platform was jam packed, it was clear there was a problem. The screen that said what time the train was coming wasn't lit up. A few moments later there was an announcement, "due to an accident, passengers travelling to Aksaya . . ." Cemil headed back to the stairs and flew up them two, three at a time. The busy traffic in Kızılay made him despair for a moment. He jumped into the first taxi he could find. But the cars on Gazi Mustafa Kemal Boulevard were caught in stop-and-go traffic. When he got to Maltepe, he looked at the clock on the display panel in the taxi: fifteen to seven. The taxi driver was talking nonstop. He was complaining about traffic, saying a smart man wouldn't try to be a taxi driver in traffic like this, explained the changes that had taken place because of cars. "But dude, I'm just crazy like that!" he said. He had done his military service as a commando in Bingöl. "If you want, I could push this car up on its side and drive us on two wheels." As he turned away from Maltepe and headed down one of the side streets, honking his horn, slamming his brakes, and making his way to Tandoğan with sharp turns, the driver said "don't worry, dude, we'll be there at seven!" At that moment Cemil thought it would be better to get out of the taxi. It made him feel like his father had when he had complained that "the doctors here are terrible!" He also felt close to his father for saying "let's go to another hospital." Cemil had quieted him down by replying "not now, Dad, not now!" The taxi driver looked at Cemil in his mirror. They were between Tandoğan and Beşevler. "Dude, honestly, let's go on two wheels, what do you say?" he asked, as if just joking, "can I close the window?" Cemil said "no need, it's fine like this." With the taxi driver swearing and honking, almost getting into an accident a few times, almost running a few people over, they arrived at the astroturf three minutes before seven. Running towards the locker room, Cemil asked himself "What am I doing? Why so much stress, why this stupid running? Am I nuts?" The locker room was locked. He went out to the field. Everyone was waiting for him. He ran to get the key from the base of the goal. Putting on his shorts and shoes in the locker room, he was drenched in sweat. He nervously tried to pee. When he got out to the field the match had already started. He made eye contact with İlhan. But then suddenly a warm whirlpool swirled around him and picked him up and carried him back and forth between the goals. Cemil gave himself over to this wonderful current. He realized why he had been so anxious and in such a hurry.

After the match, they went to eat wrapped döner pide. İlhan and Cemil didn't speak because there were people sitting around them at the same table. They both looked at each other with heads bowed.

When Cemil got home around ten, he found Nazlı eating pumpkin seeds and watching television. He told her that they had started showing *The Sultan's Melody* again during the daytime. Nazlı was sad she hadn't been able to watch it. Cemil was sad too. He showered and took an aspirin. He was too lazy to brush his teeth; he got into bed.

He still hadn't been able to get to sleep at midnight. He tossed left and right, kept thinking about his plays during the match; everything else was erased. Halfway awake, he kept trying to play what he hadn't been able to during the match on the concave field in his mind. Again and again he tried and failed. He lost the ball each time to that midfielder on the rival team who had been a professional boxer when he was young.

Cemil's unofficial list of the things that made him feel that life was a feast:

- Virginia Woolf's novel *Mrs. Dalloway*.
- The adaptation from John Cheever's story: *The Swimmer*. Directed by Frank Perry, Starring Burt Lancaster.
- Joshua Logan's film *Picnic*. Kim Novak and William Holden in the lead roles.
- Seymour Glass: Such a literary hero!
- "The Ballad of the Fallen" by Charlie Haden and Carla Bley: it wasn't a song for the fallen, it was poetry.
- Patrice Leconte's film *Monsieur Hire*. Michel Blanc in the lead role.
- Ezginin Günlüğü's album *The Boat in the Garden*.
- Mehmet Günsör's story "The Bitter End".
- Ali Osman Coşkun's paintings.
- Raymond Carver's stories, all of them.
- That folk song "Green Mirror" that Nazlı had sung while walking towards Palamutbükü.
- *I'm Overwhelmed and Leaving* by Melihat Gülses.
- Pars Tuğlacı's encyclopedic dictionary *Okyanus*.
- Wynton Marsalis' album *The Majesty of the Blues*.
- Henri Rousseau's paintings. Rousseau the customs agent.
- Led Zeppelin's *The Battle of Evermore* and their other stuff.
- *Marcovaldo or the Seasons in the City* by Italo Calvino.
- Julio Cortazar's story called "End of the Game". You know, statues and postures.
- Stevie Smith's poem "Not Waving But Drowning"; the translation by Cevat Çapan.

BARIŞ BIÇAKÇI

51

"Ms. Editor, I thought that the sentence 'he left engineering at thirty-five and committed himself to literature' would go well in my biography, so I quit my job. One of the notable perks of being petit bourgeois is the ability to imagine your own biography, and to do things merely for the sake of them being in your biography.

Mrs. Editor, surely we petit bourgeois don't only possess those luxuries we enjoy so much. We have our share of ordeals as well: ordeals like trying to understand life and others, thinking about death at every turn, looking for traces of the grandiose and the essential in small things, making generalizations, weaning off of our pleasures and feeling guilty.

Every breath we take makes us feel guilty, makes us feel like we are playing in a sandbox with our extravagances and our ordeals. One moment we're scratching around in our sandbox feeling guilty, and the next we're waiting for the real world to bring its giant fist down and smash everything we've built to smithereens. We even look forward to it. We've read Kafka, and have a real masochistic streak.

Mrs. Editor, while waiting for reality to smash its fist down, no sane person can have complete and abiding faith in anything. Not in beauty, in the good, in literature, in the world of books, in nothing . . .

I do not now myself believe, and so I ask:

What would happen if you publish my novel, what would happen if you don't?"

52

Cemil went on vacation with his friends Metin and İlhan for two weeks in October. They rented a cabin in a camping ground on the shore of a large bay in the South Aegean, just as they had done for the last sixteen years. The three of them wanted for some things in their lives to remain constant, and they were putting in the effort to make sure of it. Cemil left behind Nazlı, İlhan left his wife and child, Metin arranged his office work for the vacation and gave a key to his neighbor so they could check on his cat.

The cabin was made out of stone and wood, it had a porch, and was carefully positioned along with nine other similar cabins among the pine trees. At that time of year there was no one else in the camping ground other than daytime visitors.

They set up and went out shopping on the first day. They made a list and went to the nearby market like they always did.

They swam in the sea in the morning and spent the afternoon hours playing three-five-eight on the porch. The wind made light waves on the water that resembled a pond in the late afternoon, the sea moving to the East with nervous ripples. In the evening, they went on long walks on the seashore. When they got back they would sip on cold beer.

The view from the cabin was amazing. They watched the changing colors of the sea and sky for hours. In the evening a group of university kids who had made a day trip headed back to the city, and the campground was immersed in terrific darkness and silence. The three of them felt that there was some presence there, surrounding them there inside of the forest. The cannons fueled by propane bottles, meant to scare off the wild boars, started going off every half hour. An owl flapped its wings without making any sound. The squirrels were asleep.

It rained non-stop for two days. A man fishing with a spear came out of the water shivering in his wetsuit, his flippers making funny noises as he walked past them. Lightning struck on the opposite shore. There was the pitter-patter of rain on the roof, along with the sound of falling pinecones.

When the weather cleared, another group of young men and women came to the camp, went into the water, joked around. Their voices sounded to the three friends like the sexual chirping of birds. They were getting old.

İlhan brought up Ceren one evening while they were drinking rakı on the porch. He had stopped seeing the girl, but he was really hurting. He accused Cemil of being a coward and a hypocrite, and accused Metin of turning everything into a joke.

"Yeah," Cemil said, "I'm a coward and a hypocrite! I lust after other women too. The editor at the publishers who I gave my manuscript to. I have conversations with her in my head, and not just for literary reasons! The woman is really hot. But there is something more to it than sexual desire. I want to fall in love again."

İlhan attacked him: "Then do it!"

"I don't think I could fall in love with anybody anymore," Cemil said.

Metin said it was just pure arrogance and nothing else.

Cemil told them about Şeyda. He talked about Berkan and his efforts at writing, but never mentioned Şeyda's name. He tried to explain. "I realized something after spending time with this girl," he said, "I never spoke honestly and openly. I can't fall in love with someone I don't enjoy talking to. Don't you need a shared language, a shared sensibility in order to talk? I'm talking about the challenge of finding a shared language. That's not arrogant!"

"That's for sure," Metin said. Both of his last relationships had been with people around his age. "How could someone who didn't live through the eighties understand me?" he shouted excitedly. Then he said, "to be honest though, this is just another kind of arrogance!

What if they could understand, are we such important people that . . ." He took a deep breath and lifted his head up to the star-filled sky. "But dude, people just think they're God's gift to man. They think of themselves like they're the lead in a movie."

İlhan handed his glass to Metin. Then he turned to Cemil. He calmed down a little. "If you say you couldn't fall in love with someone you couldn't speak to, in my opinion, you're just trying to cover up a truth," he said. "You're trying to set up some arbitrary rule that will put your mind at ease as long as you stick to it."

Cemil was quiet. Just for once, could he let this go without having to respond?!

"Can you talk to Ceren?" Metin asked. She was sixteen years younger than İlhan.

"Ceren . . . " İlhan said, "just like Forugh!"

Metin said, "She's really got to you!"

"Does she even know who Forugh is?" Cemil asked.

İlhan sullenly shook his head two times. The first time nodding yes and the second shaking it no.

"We live in a world where nobody knows the same things we know anymore," Cemil said. Under the spell of the rakı, he spoke like an old man nobody liked, and one whom young people especially didn't like.

Then Forugh interrupted them: *All the lights of connection have gone out, all the lights of connection have gone out.*

Life is full of coincidences, so full of them that some days people might run into the older versions of themselves.

When Cemil came across the older version of himself in a small park in Anıttepe, he said "what a coincidence!" Cemil found himself unable to speak, and so the old Cemil started talking. Old people are always waiting for their chance to talk.

"I'm getting smaller by the day," old Cemil complained. He explained how Nazlı had to unstitch one of his shirts and take them in every day. And the collar was looking like it was too big. When he put on a hat, people had to stoop down a little bit to be able to see him. If they didn't try to stoop down then the only sign of life underneath the hat would be a nose. When old Cemil said this, he started to snicker. As soon as he finished laughing, he continued speaking at the same pace. "In the past, I used to love sitting at home. Now, I want to go out and be around people. I want to go hang out with my friends. Nazlı's nephews are quite nice hosts to us, bless them," he said. The only thing is, she can't sleep on thin pillows, she likes thick pillows. When we visit people, she has to put two pillows on top of one another, and when she wakes up in the morning, the first thing she does is change the order of the channels on the remote control to her liking. After that, she sees if the bathroom and shower hand soap are dry or not. The soap should be dry, otherwise it quickly goes bad. "They have those magnetic soap holders shaped like hands, those are really harmful I think!" she says. "They're mounted on the wall." When we go on trips, she also checks the space between the curtain rod and the window. "It bothers me if there's too much space. You know why? The warm air from the radiator gets trapped between the curtain and the glass, and the room won't heat up. It's that simple!" She starts to get really cold. Even sitting on a cold toilet seat makes her shiver. Because of that, she avoids going to the bathroom. She never wore a wristwatch in the past, but now she wants to see a clock everywhere. "On the wall, on the table, and even down there! You know what I mean?" he said, winking, a twisted smile on his lips. "Whether it's the hour hand or minute hand doesn't matter. As long as it's straight. You get it, young man, because there's a time for that?" Putting his hand down to his crotch and sticking out his pointer finger.

Cemil was turning to leave when old Cemil grabbed him by the arm. They looked at each other.

"Will you help me solve the murder?" the old Cemil asked.

Cemil is looking at the mirror and thinking about his hands. His hands are underneath a dark purple cape. His fingers are interlocked. Nervous. He unlinks his hands and moves them over his knees. Under the cape. This cape that the barber had called a bib when he wrapped it around Cemil's neck, even when it went all the way from his chin down to his knees. A bib!

Cemil still can't get something into that head of his which is being multiplied ad infinitum between the mirrors across from him: why does everything in life have to be in excess?

The metal of the faucet right in front of him is shining, water is dripping from its tip into the sink. On the counter is shaving cream, packets of blades, straight razors, shaving brushes, small plastic containers, scissors, combs, brushes, tweezers, electric razors, hair dryers, and all of these gadgets' black cables leading towards the outlet. On the shelf there are shampoo bottles, boxes of gel and wax, cologne, lotion bottles, Q-tips, and packets of cotton. On the wall, hung right over the mirror is a picture of Atatürk, diplomas, documents, and calendars from a few years ago. In the corner between the window and the wall is a television, and right underneath it a radio. Drops of rain on the glass pane. A table in front of the window, the cash register, magazines, pens, coupons. A tea kettle next to the table. A man with glasses fogged up from the steam coming from the tea kettle, a mirror behind him. Looking at the circular wall clock above the mirror it's twenty to eleven and if you turn your head it's twenty past one. Between the mirror and the door there is a cloakroom, jackets, raincoats, hats. On the floor, on the ground of the cloakroom, is an umbrella. Next to the door is an aquarium. You know, everything started there, life began in water.

"Life began in water," Cemil says.

"Yeah man," the barber says.

"The bacteria that breathes carbon dioxide and releases oxygen into the air appeared three and a half billion years ago." Cemil makes eye contact with the barber in the mirror and motions to the stupid cane plant next to the aquarium with his head. "The same bacteria that is now inside the leaves of that potted plant."

The barber looked at the stupid cane plant, unconcerned. "We spray it once in a while dude, nothing's going to happen to it!"

"Can you take a little more off the sides?" Cemil says, and thinks to himself that it's fine if people don't know anything.

It's also fine if they don't understand anything. He had thought other people understood. He thought he understood the great questions pertaining to the universe. That he had read about them and understood them. But walking around the apartment repeating to himself out loud, trying to memorize the information like a stupid student: "There was a time when all was one. Being one means being infinite. Everything was infinitely small and infinitely concentrated into one single point, and then there was a big bang. There was a big bang and matter was scattered about and brought into being, billions of galaxies, and in each one of those galaxies, billions of stars."

"Want a shampoo?" the barber asked.

Everything was scattered about, Cemil thought. The excess comes from that. Everything was scattered about, and then it contracted into itself, coming together: pulling, pushing, starting to orbit around itself. Words and sleep. Men and women. I understand. I understand, Cemil thought, that everything passes through everything else, that this jumble, this movement, the past and the future are mixing up and separating, that moments are blown around and that the mind is never ever stopping. I understand, Cemil thought as he left the barber.

He liked the feeling of raindrops on his head. The clouds were hanging really low, reaching the rooftops of the buildings, they were going to stay the night. Water was collecting on the side of the road. The cypress trees were drenched. The wind was carrying the scent of wide-open country.

It was coming again, autumn. Agitating Cemil like a mispronounced word.

"Ms. Editor, writers look for the reason behind everything, for their essence. But they know quite well that life is full of simple things that aren't worth describing. The characters they create make a special effort to describe these simple things, the daily odds and ends, the meaningless excesses, the simple things that don't seem essential that make their created worlds seem convincing, and they embrace life in the widest possible way, they try to communicate it all on paper. But then all of a sudden you hear the announcement of the death of a neighbor from the local mosque following the call to prayer. Everyone in the apartment complex listens in. Mrs. Şadiye Numan, the mother-in-law of the police officer İsmet Gönül from the Soyak block, has passed away. You get the gist of what happened, but after a brief pause, after this interruption, life disappears again into simple things, into the abundance of things not worth explaining, into itself. We'll trim our fingernails, and when we cook, we'll tilt our natural gas tank, which is almost empty, over on its side until the new one arrives, we'll clean the trap where the water hose comes in on the washing machine; while reading a book in the bathroom we'll hold our manhood in our hand so that it doesn't touch the toilet seat, we'll look for where the smell in the refrigerator is coming from: rotten dill or a jar of pickles whose lid wasn't closed all the way.

Writing consists of describing things that sort of aren't worth explaining. Daring to give meaning to the meaningless.

I will now stealthily toss out the rotten dill into the garbage before Nazlı gets home, secretly close the lid of the pickle jar, and dare once again to describe these things."

The idea to go on a hot air balloon ride was Nazlı's. She saw it on a television program about tourist destinations. Cemil was afraid, he didn't even like thinking about it. But they had to pass a test, to take stock of things. It was as though getting into a hot air balloon and going up wasn't so Nazlı could take in some panorama, but instead so she could see the years they had spent together, to see their lives.

In the last few days Cemil had fallen into despair about getting his book published and had become quite despondent. He said that the kitchen cabinet attached to the wall was too heavy; one day it was going fall on top of them. As Nazlı was putting away plates and glasses on the shelf, he appeared in the kitchen doorway, anxiously shaking his head. "A huge cabinet, held up by just a couple of screws!" Nazlı didn't pay attention to him, she was afraid of something else. In her childhood there was a hill covered in daisies where she used to walk barefoot. From the top of that hill she would look out at her grandmother's dark wood house among others like it, and at other hills, the large ash trees full of leaves, and the clouds. She was afraid that this was a childhood memory, and nothing more. She said she wanted to plant a tree, to work in the soil. She would walk barefoot again to the top of the hills, and call out to the daisies "I am so alone! Now that I am one of you I am so alone."

Then one day she suggested they go on a tour with her doctor friends. Cemil refused. He hated being a tourist. He said tourism was an activity reserved for hypocritical members of the bourgeoisie. He made exaggerated tourist-like gestures, and Nazlı smiled joylessly. On another day she said "I want to see Cappadocia! I want to go on a hot air balloon ride." Her eyes were teary. Cemil couldn't resist. They both felt it.

They left on a bus full of doctors and nurses. There were conversations and laughter. There was even singing. Nazlı and Cemil looked at each other. Cemil stood up and made a buck-tooth grin and asked, "would you still love me if I was ugly like this?" The people on the bus were surprised, there was a pause. Nazlı smiled as she looked out the window. Right after checking into the hotel, almost everyone in the group split up. They went off to explore different places, they didn't show up to the group lunches and dinners. They didn't complain about the tour guide, they didn't praise the wide selection of items at the breakfasts. The young women and men in the group didn't flirt with each other. They retreated into their rooms early in the evening. Cemil worried that the shelf fixed to the wall wouldn't be able to hold the weight of the television. Nazlı ate bran biscuits.

They both felt it.

One afternoon they went to get information about a hot air balloon tour. Cemil had assumed that Nazlı would let the whole thing go, but she was adamant. The hot air balloon baskets were cute, it looked like they were going to take them to a picnic in the sky. The guides explained the tour with smiles on their faces, inspiring confidence. As the balloon was readied they would be treated to breakfast, and when they landed they would get champagne. As well they would get a certificate for having participated in a flight.

"A certificate?" Cemil asked.

The view was amazing. There wasn't a cloud in the sky. The ground below looked like a playground. When Cemil worked up the courage and looked out at what Nazlı was looking at, he could see a fertile valley covered in all sorts of autumnal colors, stretching out in-between a rugged and barren landscape. They started descending around the fairy chimneys. The dark shadow of the balloon grazed the fairy chimneys. Nazlı and Cemil first looked at their own shadows being cast over the fairy chimneys and then at each other. Nazlı smiled, felt embarrassed for smiling, even got a little mad at herself. She tried not to smile. But she smiled again, and again. She leaned her head forward and snuggled it against Cemil. Cemil hung on close to his wife and took in the scent he had known for years along with the morning air. He took in a deep breath.

They both felt it.

57

"Ms. Editor, Balzac said that art was nature concentrated. He had it right. If the world hadn't contained someone named Nazlı, if I had never met her, if I had never fallen in love with her, I would have no doubt kissed Balzac on the forehead, and closed all of the doors, and gladly given permission for my nature to be concentrated."

58

Fall was trying to give shape to a metallic, contorted sorrow. When at last it succeeded, a dark silence reigned over the apartment complex area, and Cemil heard a "click!" sound. He got up from the table to try to see where the sound was coming from. He stopped and listened in the doorway to the living room. There was no sound. He went into the bathroom and looked at the drop ceiling, in the bedroom, the kitchen. No sound. He turned his head back to the table and the book he was reading and again heard the "click!"

Right after that the telephone rang.

The editor introduced herself, asked how he was. She said that they hadn't been able to take a look at his literary manuscript for the last six months.

Cemil only said "yes."

"I want to start out by saying that, in general, I liked your manuscript," the editor said. "Your language, your style, it's very very good. In some parts you've attained an extremely poetic style. Not something you often come across in prose. That being said, we have some suggestions for the novel's protagonist."

"I'm listening," Cemil said, thinking that the novel wouldn't be published. CPR would be of no use.

"We find your character hard to believe. Yes, he's a good and ethical person. But we barely see him in action. It makes us begin to doubt his goodness and his ethics. We even doubt that he's real." The editor paused for a moment. Cemil thought she must be quickly rubbing her thumb and forefinger together. "You need to mussy up your characters a little. Make them do something wrong, make them bad. Isn't that the way it is in real life? We do things even though we know they're wrong, don't we? Your protagonist is such a clean-cut guy that . . . It's like it's not a real life, but instead a show being put on. I mean to say, it gives you a certain feeling when you're reading it. Do you know what I mean? Too naive. You have to break that, you have to mussy it up a little."

"Yes," Cemil said.

"Look at it like this and go back to your writing . . . if you go back over it . . . believe me it will really enrich the text. Because your language is sound. But the character . . ."

Cemil said "Of course, of course."

"In that case we look forward to a new draft of your manuscript," the editor said, seeming relieved. "But please, there's no rush!"

After hanging up the phone, Cemil started wandering around the apartment. He wandered around unconsciously. He looked at the button for the light switch on the exhaust fan above the stove, he looked at the shoe horn, and at the sponge, at the paint stains on the curtains in the living room, looked out through the peephole and called Nazlı.

Nazlı tried to calm Cemil down. "What will you do now?"

"I have no idea," Cemil said, "I guess I need to think a little, I need to calm down, come to my senses. I don't know, I'm in a bad way. Like the floor has been pulled out from underneath me . . ."

When he said this, Nazlı's voice got shaky, like a mother whose child had gotten sick or fallen down, who felt sorry that they were hurt but was also secretly angry: "Why are you taking this so seriously? So what if they rejected it! If you want to make those changes then do it, if you don't then don't . . . You're very ambitious Cemil, you've attached a lot of significance to that book. You've worked yourself into a corner. I think if you listen to Seymour's story about Bananafish you'll feel better!"

Nazlı's words tore Cemil out by the roots, hurting him badly. He hung up the phone and started wandering around the apartment again like a dandelion seed. He shuttled between the bedroom and the living room. He stopped at the bathroom door. He stopped in front of the mirror in the entryway. He looked out through the peephole at the door of the apartment across from them. Then he went into the kitchen, leaned against the counter, and stared at the trivet hanging on the wall. Suddenly he heard the "click!" sound again. It was coming from the large glass bowl on the counter in which Nazlı had been soaking chickpeas that morning. She hadn't taken them out. He put his elbows on the counter, rested his chin on the palms of his hands. He got close to the chickpeas, swollen up in the water, and looked, and looked . . .

"Alright!" he said, emphasizing the last syllable as though it were a term of endearment.